Last Chance Summer

Last Chance Summer

Diana J. Wieler

A Prairie Book
Published by
Douglas & McIntyre Ltd.
Toronto/Vancouver

Copyright © 1986 by Diana Wieler
First mass market edition 1992

Second printing 1994

This book was published originally by Western
Producer Prairie Books, a book publishing
venture owned by the Saskatchewan Wheat
Pool.

Douglas & McIntyre Ltd.
585 Bloor Street West
Toronto, Ontario   M6G 1K5

The publisher acknowledges the support
received for this publication from the Canada
Council and the Saskatchewan Arts Board.

Canadian Cataloguing in Publication Data

Wieler, Diana J. (Diana Jean), 1961–
    Last chance summer

ISBN 1-55054-225-7

I. Title.

PS8595.I44L38 1992   jC813'.54   C92-094926-6
PZ7.W54La 1992

Cover illustration by Oni
Cover design by Warren Clark/GDL
Printed and bound in Canada

For Lorraine Blashill, with admiration and appreciation

1

The detective steered the boy into the tiny office and pushed him firmly into a chair.

"I don't need to get out the cuffs, do I, Marl?" the detective said, his hands still clamped securely around the boy's shoulders. It wasn't a question, it was an order: Don't run, don't move. Without looking up, Marl shook his head. There was no fight left in him now. He'd spent it all in the two-block race he'd run with the detective. Run and lost.

Walking around the desk, the detective saw the boy in full light for the first time. Nothing he'd seen under the street lamps or in the squad car prepared him; a shiver ran down his spine. Marl was twelve, but he was hunched in the chair like an old man. His brown hair, the color of strong coffee, hung in straggly clumps around his neck and over his eyes. After three days on the street anyone would be grimy, but there was a darkness about the boy that wasn't dirt. The hollows under his eyes and cheekbones couldn't be washed away.

"When did you eat last?" the detective asked. "Are you hungry?"

Marl shrugged and the detective opened a drawer and pulled out a sandwich, still enclosed in its plastic triangle. It was meant to be his 3 A.M. snack, but he dropped it on the desk in front of the boy. Marl didn't touch it. The detective's breath ran out in a small sigh as he reached for the phone.

Marl hated police stations and he especially hated them at night. It was past 2 A.M., Marl could see by the detective's watch, and the fluorescent lights made everything seem stark and grim and faintly gray. The detective's face looked sickly, blue around the edges. Marl could guess what his own face looked like.

"Miss Martin? This is Detective Stanbuck of Juvenile calling," the officer said into the receiver. Marl's body tensed and his stomach lurched. He was listening so hard the back of his neck prickled.

'We have it on record that Marl Silversides is one of your . . . clients," the detective continued. "Well, we found him. He's in custody now." There was a pause; Marl could almost hear Cecile Martin's voice and he could imagine the worry in it.

"Oh, he's fine," the detective said, looking at Marl. "Nothing that a little soap and water won't cure. And rest, and a good meal." Detective Stanbuck listened again; Marl's ears strained.

"Good," the officer said, "we'll be waiting. Someone at the information desk will help you find us." Then he hung up the phone.

Relief washed over Marl in a wave. She was coming, Cecile was coming for him! He'd been afraid that this would be the last straw, that she'd give up on him. He'd been afraid that Family Services would assign another social worker to him, someone tougher, someone stricter. Someone who wasn't Cecile. But she was coming.

The relief was quickly replaced by anxiety. What was he going to say when Cecile asked why he'd run away *this* time? How could he explain another broken promise? He'd broken so many that one more shouldn't matter, but it did. Marl clenched his hands and his fingernails dug into his palms. The worst part about running away wasn't getting caught; it wasn't the late-night police stations or the trip back to Juvenile Court. It was looking into Cecile's

2

face, seeing the disappointment in her brown eyes, knowing he'd let her down. Again.

Marl's feet were swinging underneath the chair, the way they always did when he was nervous. He ran his hand across his forehead, trying to wipe off some of the grime. He knew the detective was watching him curiously but he didn't care. He was just about to ask if he could go to the bathroom when there was a quiet knock and the door swung open.

Marl looked up. Cecile's short curly hair hadn't been combed and she was wearing jeans and an old T-shirt. Marl still thought she was the prettiest woman he'd ever known.

"Hi," Cecile said. "Long time no see."

"Hi," Marl said, his voice sounding small and strange. There was an awkward silence until Detective Stanbuck rose.

"I'll give you some privacy," he said. "I'll be out in the hall if you need me."

As soon as she and Marl were alone, Cecile took a deep breath to steady herself. Three days! she thought. Had he only been out on the street that long? From the way he looked, it could have been three weeks. Marl was a compact boy, small even for a twelve-year-old, and now he seemed wasted. Cecile wanted to throw her arms around him and hug him tightly. She also wanted to shake him until he promised never to run away again.

She did neither. Instead she walked over and sat down in another chair, facing Marl.

"How ya doin'?" she asked. "Where'd you go?"

"I was around," Marl said. "Eighth Avenue mostly." Cecile shuddered. Eighth Avenue was a paved outdoor walking mall that attracted the homeless by the hundred. Bag-ladies, runaways, unkempt old men, young people with glassy, burned-out eyes. It was the most dangerous street in the city.

"What happened with the Harcourts?" Cecile asked. They were the people Marl had been staying with, a reg-

3

ular family that took in "difficult" children on a short-time basis. "They seemed like nice people."

Marl knew about Nice People. They were everywhere: their blue eyes flashed on T.V. and their clean hair shone in magazines. Nice People had mothers and fathers and sisters and brothers and grandparents. They lived on tree-lined streets and went on family picnics. Nice People had each other and they stuck together. They didn't need Marl Silversides, and he knew it.

"It didn't work out," Marl said, shifting restlessly in his seat.

"I gathered that."

"Their kids were pickin' on me, 'cause of my color," Marl offered.

Marl had gentle doe-brown skin that turned darker in the sun. He also had almond-shaped eyes that were very different from any he saw on the perfect faces of Nice People. At ten, Marl had been interested in his ancestry and had peered into a mirror every chance he got. His exotic, slanted eyes puzzled him.

"Maybe there was this Chinese guy in there somewhere," he had said to Cecile.

"Maybe," she'd replied kindly, but Cecile had seen those eyes too many times on too many faces. She'd seen his lips too, slightly puffy and rounded. It was all part of a condition that had another name, but what it meant was that Marl's mother had drunk heavily while she was pregnant and stacked the cards against a kid she would never know.

Cecile knew him, though, and she knew when he was trying to con her. Despite any trouble he had with school-work, Marl was not dumb. He was actually very bright; even his former social worker had mentioned that to her, when she had first taken him on. It was only his appearance and his reading ability that had been affected; he was observant and ingenious, and he was trying his luck with her right now.

4

"Nice try, Marl," she said, "but you've used that color story before. What's the real reason you took off?"

The boy squirmed uncomfortably. After two years there was no faking it with Cecile: She could read his face like a report card. Marl shrugged and stared at his hands, his feet swinging faster under the chair.

Cecile sighed.

"We're trying to help you, kid, but you're not letting us. I had to work real hard to get you in with the Harcourts. You've taken off so many times that Family Services gives me a dirty look if I even mention a foster home now."

She drummed her fingers softly on the desk.

"I can get you into the children's shelter tonight, but after that, I don't know. I'll level with you, Marl. This could mean closed custody at Ryerson."

Marl had been at Ryerson, the boys' institution, and he'd known guys who'd been in closed custody. The kids called it "C.C." It meant being confined to your tiny room when you weren't at classes. It meant no outings, no privileges. C.C. was what they did when they had given up hope on you, when they just wanted to keep you off the streets until you were old enough to become somebody else's problem. With wire mesh on the windows and rooms with locks on the *outside*, Ryerson could be like a prison. A month, even a day there, could be a long, long time.

When Cecile left the room to speak to the detective, she left the door open. Marl heard the soft patter of slippers on tile and looked up to see a cleaning lady wiping the door jamb with a rag. The lights were too bright, he thought, thrusting his grimy hands into his pockets. The woman stared at him, as if he were a smudge against the clean, white wall. Marl looked away.

How could he tell Cecile what it was like? She'd asked again and again if people were unkind to him. Marl had to admit that they weren't, not usually.

"Well, what is it then?" she'd asked. That was the part

5

he couldn't explain. How could he describe something that was only a dull ache in the pit of his stomach, and a feeling of choking when he wasn't choking at all?

Marl had dreams, and he couldn't tell Cecile about those either. She would have thought he was crazy. Just remembering them made Marl's throat tighten and his breath come in gasps.

It was always the same dream, a dream of a train. Marl had never been on a train in real life. He'd never even been close to one, but he'd seen them in movies and on T.V. Marl's train was huge, black and ominous. It clanked metal and hissed steam, belching black smoke and rumbling over the prairie as unstoppable as thunder. Marl didn't know how far the boxcars went back because he was in the cab with the engineer.

In his dream, it was night, a swallowing blackness that only the prairies know. The cab of the train was lit with eerie swinging lanterns that threw a devilish glow on the grim face of the engineer. A few other people were there, sitting against the walls, swaying in rhythm with the train. Their faces were as stern as prison wardens' and when they looked at him, he could feel his hands sweat. They knew what he had done. The train clanked and chugged through the darkness for a long time.

"Isn't it morning yet?" Marl asked desperately, his voice only a squeak. "Isn't morning coming yet?"

The people stared back at him blankly and the grizzled engineer said nothing. Marl's stomach was knotting. The train was moving so fast!

Suddenly, he heard it, a sharp whistle in the distance. Marl leapt to his feet and looked out the front window. There was a light glowing far down the tracks but it wasn't dawn. It was another train.

"Wait!" Marl cried, tugging the engineer's sleeve. "Stop! You've got to stop!"

The engineer didn't even look at him. The train was picking up speed. Marl glanced out the window again and realized with horror that the brilliant, dangerous light was getting closer and closer! Frantic, he reached to shake the engineer's sleeve, but the man was gone, as were the people who'd been in the cab. He was alone and he couldn't stop the train!

"Jump!" Marl's heart cried to him, but when he looked up through the window the white beam of the other train caught him and held him. The trains thundered towards each other and Marl couldn't look away. He couldn't move to save himself. A hundred yards, fifty. The deadly glow filled the cab and still Marl clutched the handrail, blinded, helpless. A whistle screamed in his ears . . .

. . . and he would wake, gasping.

In his dark room, Marl would shake, wiping his sweat and tears of fright on the sheet. His stomach would be knotted in the familiar clenching pain, an ache that followed the dreams like the dreams followed Marl. No matter where he went, no matter how hard he tried to fit in, the dream found him. Laying his forehead on his knees, Marl would gently rock himself to sleep. He would know it was time to go.

When Marl was settled in at the children's shelter, Cecile drove home and made herself a pot of coffee, curling up at the window to watch the paling sky. She knew it was no use trying to sleep. Cecile had ten other juvenile clients to worry about, but Marl was the one that haunted her.

Why, why this one? she wondered to herself, but all she kept seeing was Marl's diamond-shaped face and his odd, slanted eyes. When Cecile was in college training to be a social worker, the problem kids were classified as "outward-hurting" and "inward-hurting." Outward-hurting children were the vandals, the kids who broke into houses, went on shooting sprees, or fought bloody battles in the streets. They splattered their anger as far as they could hurl it. The inward-hurting children were the heavy drug users, the runaways, the prostitutes. They were the "rippers." "Ripping" was a Ryerson term. It was what some kids did with knives to their forearms or the calves of their legs in times of stress. The social workers Cecile knew called the groups "innies" and "outties," like belly buttons. Marl was an innie.

He wasn't a good risk for a foster home anymore: No one would recommend him. That left only Ryerson Hall and the thought of it made Cecile shiver. In the rough-and-tumble pack at Ryerson, only the strong, aggressive kids survived. The innies were the casualties.

There was someplace else, a group home located on a farm an hour's drive out of the city. It was run by an Englishman named Carleton Jenner and Cecile's colleagues thought he was a little strange. Cecile had overheard their comments.

"Runs the whole farm by himself,"one social worker said. "Nine tough kids to him and a housekeeper. What's he aiming for—a sainthood?"

"Either that or a nervous breakdown," said another worker. "I know some of those kids."

Cecile worried about how Marl would fare, thrown in with a group like that. But could it be any worse than Ryerson? Could it be any lonelier than closed custody? Besides, she'd heard that the farm had a good success rate; fewer boys were in trouble after they reached legal age and had left the farm.

She'd also met Carleton Jenner once, at a conference. He'd had a brightness about him, a warmth that she noticed when he spoke about "his lads." Some people called Carleton "possessive," but Cecile understood that. It was a trait she was always being warned about herself.

"You can't devote so much time to this one boy," the director of Family Services had told her. "Cecile, don't be so possessive. Marl is a ward of the court."

But he's *my* Marl too, Cecile thought, now as she looked out at the rising sun. That made a difference.

With these thoughts on her mind she rose and walked over to a file of index cards she kept by the phone. It was filled with names and numbers of social agencies. It also held the business card Carleton Jenner had pressed into her hand at the conference. She remembered his words clearly.

"If you ever need anything," he'd said, his blue eyes bright and earnest, "just give me a ring."

She needed him now, for Marl. Cecile took a deep breath and began to dial.

2

The Jenner farm wasn't a real one, just a large house with a few ramshackle buildings scattered around it. The first owner had been a farmer, but he'd sold off his land piece by piece, until all that remained were three acres. They were untended now and looked as if they'd been plunked down in the middle of the wheatfields by mistake. There were other mistakes on this part of the prairie: great gaping canyons that had dry valleys, dusty and scruffy as desert. When the early settlers first arrived, they'd seen the dead valleys surrounded by the good earth of the plains, and scratched their heads, wondering. They named it the Badlands and no one had found reason to call it anything else.

On his drive from the city, Marl didn't see the impressive part of the Badlands. The valleys were fifteen miles beyond the Jenner place so all the boy saw were the fields, an endless green carpet of spring wheat. They frightened him. The prairie seemed so open and wild it took his breath and his words away. His whole first day in the Jenner household, Marl kept to himself and said nothing. On his second day, he almost got his head kicked in.

"It wasn't my fault," Marl thought later, his almond eyes narrowing. "*He* should have known better."

That he was Carleton Jenner, who knew a great many things but not that Marl didn't know how to hoe a garden.

Carleton was a busy man and he looked it. His long, skinny legs could take great strides, moving him across the farm at surprising speed. It was a pace he had learned as a schoolboy in England: The headmaster there had frowned on dawdling. Now Carleton seemed to hurry everywhere.

He had the hands of a pianist, but he did not play. Instead his long fingers grasped a thickly padded clipboard as he wrote notes to himself.

"Kevin seems depressed today," the notes might say, or, "Cal really has a knack for building things."

At night, Carleton would read over his scribblings in his tiny office, transferring anything important into a daily journal he kept. Occasionally he shared the notes with the boys' social workers, but not often. Carleton considered the goings-on at the farm to be a private matter, "just between me and the lads," as he would comment to himself.

Along with the notes there was always a copy of the day's roster on the clipboard. It was a list of the chores which had to be done that day, and who were to do them. Another copy of the roster hung in the kitchen and on it Marl saw his name. It was written right next to "Hoeing the Potato Garden."

He stared at the roster dully. Marl had never hoed a garden. He'd never even planted a seed or pruned a bush. He always got nervous when he had to try something he'd never done before. What if he couldn't do it? Part of him wanted just to go off somewhere and pretend he hadn't seen the roster at all. But he couldn't do that either.

"You will try, won't you, Marl?" Cecile had said, holding both his arms so that he would look at her. "You will try to get along?"

How could he do anything but promise with her right there like that? When he was close to Cecile, something in Marl really wanted to be good, really wanted to try.

Her eyes were the warmest color of brown that there was, and they stayed with him. He set off to find the potato garden.

Someone was already there. He was tall and sturdy looking, with chestnut hair that glinted red in the sun. He wore a checked shirt that looked tight across the shoulders, as if he'd grown from the time he'd put it on. The boy was slashing the earth with a hoe, hacking away at clump after clump of dirt. He seemed to know what he was doing.

The sun was hot on the back of Marl's neck and he began to sweat. His dark eyes were squinted, partly because of the glaring light and partly because Marl didn't want anyone to see them. He knew that if someone could see your eyes, they could see right inside you. Marl felt small and scared and dumb, and he didn't want anyone to see that inside him, ever.

The boy's name was Topo. He was thirteen but looked older. The harsh Badlands sun had already burned the fair skin on his arms and face and it made him look angry. In truth, Topo *was* angry. Out of the corner of his eye he saw the new kid who was standing stupidly at the edge of the long garden, watching him work. The hoeing had to be finished by noon and the sight of Marl doing nothing rubbed against Topo, like a pebble in his shoe. He stood up crossly.

"Well, don't just stand there, twerp," Topo barked. "Get your hoe and move dirt!"

Marl flinched and his sweaty hands clenched into fists. He hated it when people called him names but he didn't think he wanted to fight about it. Topo's arms were twice the size of Marl's and his shoulders were broad and muscular. With a grimace, Marl sauntered to the wall and picked up his hoe awkwardly. That was at nine o'clock.

By eleven o'clock sweat had soaked the back of his yellow T-shirt and the long, heavy hoe had rubbed his hands raw. Just moving his fingers made them ache and Marl stood up often, to ease the pain in his neck and back.

Hoeing was the hardest work he could ever remember doing.

Topo, whose back was already strong and whose hands were covered with calluses, did not feel Marl's pain. He felt only the burning sun, which irritated him, and thought only that he was working much harder than the new kid.

I always get stuck with the useless babies, Topo simmered to himself. I always have to do the most work. He struck at the earth savagely with his hoe but the feeling grew inside him, rumbling and snarling. The more he tried to hold it back, the bigger and uglier it became. Finally, it overflowed.

"Hey punk," he said, straightening up and wiping the sweat out of his eyes, "you're useless, y'know? Why don't you get off your butt and do something?"

At that moment, Marl had been swinging the hoe as hard as he could, gritting his teeth as the blisters on his tender hands were torn apart. Topo's words stung like a slap. Marl spun around and almost bumped into the other boy, who was suddenly close. Rough and calloused, Topo seemed bigger and stronger than a thirteen-year-old could ever be. His huge arms gleamed with sweat. Marl could feel the heat from Topo's body and smell the harsh salt on his skin.

Marl's eyes darkened. He's testing me, he thought; he's pushing me to see how far I'll let him go.

Marl had been tested before. At Ryerson, everyone had scuffled and fought for rank, to see who could push who around. Once they knew they could rattle you, they never let up. Never. Marl's jaw tensed and his hands gripped even more tightly around the handle of the hoe.

"Stuff it," he said.

Topo's head jerked up in surprise, but then he began to smile. Even though Marl had a hoe, he knew he could break the small boy. Also, Marl was the one with a weapon: Topo could tell them he had been attacked.

"Say it again," he whispered menacingly. A lump lodged

in Marl's throat and his heart pounded in his ears. He couldn't back down now.

The fury came from nowhere. Topo saw only a denim shirt flash by him and Marl felt his arm being jerked hard, almost out of its socket. The hoe flew onto the dirt and Marl found himself hurtling over the garden, suddenly rounding a corner and being flung into a shed. When the door slammed behind them, the darkness was suffocating. Marl's side ached. He trembled with relief, panting and listening to the other gasp for breath.

Light filtered through the cracks in the wooden shed where the boards had not been laid together properly, and gradually Marl's eyes began to adjust. He recognized the boy who had saved him from Topo. Marl had heard the others call him Goat. It was a strange name but then, from what Marl had seen, Goat was strange.

He was wide across the shoulders but bony, and his blonde hair was spiky, very goat like. Marl knew that Goat was fourteen, the oldest of the boys on the farm. He did look older, but exhausted somehow, as if fourteen years in the same body had worn his skin right to the bones. He had a scar too: a pale white line between his nose and cheekbone, on the right side of his face. The scar made Marl wonder.

The figure leaned to his left and spit. "You're so dumb," Goat gasped and swallowed. "You almost got your head kicked in."

Marl leaned shakily against a shelf. In the half-light he knew Goat couldn't see the tremors.

"I would have had him," he answered bravely, thrusting his chin out a bit. "He isn't so big."

Goat glanced sideways at Marl and a sliver of light shone on the scar on his face. He looked away and Marl knew that Goat didn't believe him. Silence settled down with the dust.

"He led you into that," Goat said finally, still not looking at Marl. "If Jenner had been around, *you* would have caught it. You were the one with a weapon. They would have shipped you off and Topo would have been laughing."

Dully, Marl realized that Goat was right, but he couldn't let down his front.

"So?" he answered jauntily. "This place stinks, anyhow. I'd like to get out of here."

Goat let a gaping pause hang in the air and Marl fidgeted uncomfortably. Why did he feel so nervous?

"Watch yourself, kid," Goat said slowly, and he spit. "I don't want to have to save your ass again."

A blinding flash of sunlight hit Marl in the eyes as the door opened. Then he was left alone in the strangling heat.

Goat was walking with his shoulders hunched, his hands dug deep into his pockets. He was too angry to care where he was going.

"Dumb kid," he muttered to himself, "dumb, twerpy little kid."

He couldn't remember when he'd been so irritated and not knowing the reason for it only made it worse.

"If he had half a brain, he would have known Topo could kick his teeth in," Goat said aloud. "I should have let him do it."

But even as he thought about it, Goat knew he didn't mean it. Marl was just a kid; Topo was a half-grown man, dangerously bitter and angry. You didn't live with Topo, you lived around him—if you wanted any peace at all.

The weight was pressing down on Goat's shoulders again and the pain clamped around his neck like a vise. His feet dragged from a tiredness that he couldn't escape.

What was it, he wondered, that bugged him so much about the dark-eyed boy, and fascinated him so that he stared at Marl and couldn't look away? He had been watching Marl since he'd come and when he'd seen the boy out in the garden with Topo . . . well, he suddenly felt sorry for him. His feet had moved before he could think about it.

15

But now he was mad, angry with Marl for making him break through the comfortable cocoon he'd woven around himself. Goat had grown tired of feeling a long time ago. Being numb was safer, it kept him in control. But it was a full-time job and sometimes he forgot to forget, or he just didn't have the energy anymore. Then the cloud as dark as a prairie storm would overwhelm him, and exhaustion would win.

It was winning now. Goat's eyelids flickered over his gray-blue eyes, the color of a rainy sea. His feet had found their way back to the farmhouse and they carried him straight up to his room.

When Goat didn't show up for lunch, Carleton Jenner ran lightly up the stairs to check. He found the scruffy figure stretched out on his stomach, his arms wrapped tightly around his head.

"System overload," Carleton said softly to himself. Goat was like that. Sometimes, just *being* was such an effort that the boy shut down whenever it became too much. Carleton had seen him fall asleep while eating, while watching T.V., and once even while painting a fence.

"It's good to see that he's simmered down," Goat's social worker had said to Carleton, but the Englishman knew better. Goat's energy was being drained away by something and looking at the skinny boy, you knew there wasn't much left to take. Carleton padded quietly down to the kitchen, trying not to bring his worried frown back o the table.

3

Lunchtime seemed endless to Marl. It was hard on his ears, which strained for the mention of his name, and hard on his eyes, which darted cautiously, keeping track of the new faces. Marl had been careful not to sit next to the big, sunburned boy at the long wooden table, but he didn't sit too far away, either. He didn't want Topo, or anyone else, to think he was scared.

But no one noticed Marl. They were too busy. They boys threw fried potatoes, jostled elbows, and pinched and poked whoever wasn't looking. They tilted back in their chairs, kicked under the table, clattered the silverware, and yelled threats at one another so that the place was more like a circus than a dining room.

"Watch your goddamned elbows! Keep 'em on your own side."

"Just shut up, already."

"Oh, gross."

Clang! A pot lid crashed down on the table and Marl jumped back in surprise. It was Vilda the cook, angry and sweaty, her hands curled into fists on her wide hips.

"I said ENOUGH," she barked. "I'm not tellin' you again." She swivelled to Marl's left and raised a threatening forefinger.

"You fling one more potato, Len, and you're gonna wear 'em. And you," she said to a thin, curly haired boy named

Cal, "you elbow Brucie again and by God, I'll chain you to that chair. Don't give me those innocent eyes!"

Vilda was no beginner. She'd had children of her own, although she never talked about them. Looking at her, Marl couldn't have guessed *when* she might have had them. Vilda's hair should have been gray, but it wasn't. It was an electric blue-black that clashed with her pale skin and faded freckles. She tried to keep it back, but her hair flew out in kinky strands, giving her a wild look. Vilda was shaped like a tired squash: Everything drooped towards the bottom. But Marl wasn't fooled. Vilda's eyes were alert and she was an expert with her wooden spoon. Before lunch, it had landed across Cal's knuckles.

Now she flicked back a sweaty lock of her hair and glared at them.

"Don't push your luck," she warned, and turned back to a huge pot she had simmering on the stove, still keeping an eye on them from the kitchen. There were a few smirks and the noise began again, but much more quietly. Vilda was clearly a cook to be reckoned with.

Marl went back to chewing quietly and listening. He was still waiting for Topo to complain or make some snide remark about him. It didn't happen. Marl guessed that the muscular boy didn't want to come across like a crybaby. He didn't know that as far as revenge was concerned, Topo was patient. He could let it go—until the time was right. People like Topo never forgave and never forgot. They just waited.

Marl had also been worried that someone would tell Mr. Jenner he hadn't finished his job in the garden. But if the Englishman knew, he never mentioned it to Marl. He came up afterwards, when Marl was on table-clearing duty, and asked him how he was getting along. Without looking up, Marl mumbled that things were okay. Carleton patted Marl's shoulder in a solid, good-natured way.

"Good, good lad! Glad to have you aboard," he sang crisply. Then in three strides his long legs took him out of the room.

Cecile came by that evening, on her own time, and Marl waited nervously while she talked with Mr. Jenner in his office. He wondered what they were talking about, what plans they might be making.

When you're a kid, they don't have to tell you anything, he thought.

Maybe he had to go to Ryerson after all. Maybe the director didn't want to take any more chances with him. Marl shuddered. Even the burnt, Badlands prairie was better than that.

He breathed a sigh of relief when Cecile emerged, her dark face shining with a smile. She had obviously heard something she liked, although Marl couldn't guess what it might be. He showed her the room he shared with two other boys and Cecile admired the view.

Marl was over at the bureau, opening drawers.

"And this is where I keep my stuff," he said, rooting around and pulling out a T-shirt as if to prove it. "I got three drawers of my own and that shelf over there."

"Marl," Cecile said, as the hope buoyed in her, bobbing to the surface. All the emotion she tried to hold down bubbled out in the word. "Marl,"

The boy turned, still clutching his shirt. He'd heard the hope, and it ignited his own. For an instant anything was possible.

This time, he wanted to tell Cecile, this time it'll be okay. I've got this feeling and if everybody just stays out of my way, I'll be as good as I know how. Then maybe it'll be okay.

But he didn't know how to say it and the words couldn't get past his throat. The feeling was so strong he was afraid his voice would break. So he stood there, feeling hopeful and staring, until a strand of his long bangs slipped and got caught in his eyelashes, making him blink.

Cecile laughed and the tension fell away.

"Time for a haircut," she said lightly. "I'll come back before my holidays and give everyone a good scalping."

"Oh, thanks a lot," Marl groaned and Cecile threw a

pillow at him. Marl felt better than he had in a long time.

Fifteen minutes after Cecile was gone somebody pulled the plug and all the hope swirled like water down a bathtub drain.

"Hey, ugly!" a voice whispered behind him, "Who pinned your ears back for ya?"

Marl swung around. He'd been on his way to the kitchen for a glass of orange juice. In the darkened hallway he could see it was Len, the fried potato–flinger.

Len was a tawny-haired boy with a sharp edge to his chin and a hard glint to his eyes. He was older than Marl, but not as old as Goat, and he had a playful side that wasn't fun at all. He wore gold-rimmed glasses and he was smart. Len liked to play his own kind of games.

"Hey, ugly," the voice repeated, "You know who tied the elastic around your head?" He pulled back the skin around his eyes, flattening them into slits.

The words stabbed at Marl like little knives. There was always someone to remind him every day that he was different, that he was strange. His stomach rolled and his face burned. The left side of Marl's mouth crumpled into a disgusted sneer.

"Shut your face," he said, and Len's arm shot out, knocking him backwards. He slammed into the wall but lunged forward, red with rage. Len's glasses flew and they were at each other, grabbing, kicking, punching. The telltale sounds reached Carleton in his study.

"Oh no," the Englishman breathed and dashed down the hallway to pry them apart. They struggled but the thin man was strong.

"Hey, hey lads! What's ado? What's this on about here?"

Coldly, Len bent down to retrieve his glasses which had plastic lenses so they didn't break. Then he glared silently at the other boy until Carleton looked into the dark almond eyes that had been the start of the trouble.

"Marl?" he asked. Marl, whose good night had been ruined forever was left with only a bitter taste in his mouth. He flung a few choice words at Len, then a couple at Carleton Jenner for good measure.

Carleton let go of Len's arm and grasped Marl's shirt-front firmly with both hands.

"I think," he said calmly, "you'd better spend some time by yourself, laddie." Each word was steady and carried clear, controlled strength. "It'll give you a chance to think."

He'd been holding Marl up on tiptoe and now he let him back down with careful precision. Marl pulled away as if he'd been burned and ran to his room, a dull thud thud in his ears.

Never! It was never going to work, not here, not anywhere. Things were so wrong they couldn't be fixed. There would never be a place for him, where he would just be another kid, where he could fit in. He'd gotten his hopes up, that was the problem. Marl knew that whenever you started thinking that maybe you'd work out okay, God or whoever had to push you back down. It was already decided what would happen. He couldn't change it.

Marl stared out the window at the prairie night sky and far away he heard the piercing cry of a siren. But it could have been a train.

Downstairs, Carleton Jenner sat in his study, his long, sensitive fingers interlocked as he leaned forward at the desk. He'd had Len in for a "chat" but learned nothing. Len was a perfect example of what a clever kid could do to the system that was trying to help him. He'd been around social workers and therapists so long that he knew all the escape routes.

"I was having an emotional crisis," Len said, picking a thread off his shirt-sleeve. "I was reacting to a guilt burden left over from my broken home."

"Rubbish," Carleton answered shortly.

"Just ask Jim," Len said and he smiled a bit. Jim was Len's worker and not a bad fellow, but he was very new. Jim listened intently to every word that came out of Len's mouth and looked at the serious hazel eyes behind the gold-rimmed glasses. Len was so convincing that it was hard for Jim to believe the boy could be such a trouble maker.

Carleton knew better. He had been around longer and he could see right through someone like Len. But he couldn't do a thing about it. The boys' social workers had the final say when it came to overall strategy. Even if Carleton made suggestions, no one had to follow them. That meant there was no winning with a kid like Len, and the boy knew it.

"Out," Carleton motioned tiredly. Enjoying himself, Len yawned and stretched and sauntered to the door, pausing to give Carleton one last superior smile. For a crazy moment the Englishman wished he had a plant pot to fling as the door closed.

What am I going to do? he wondered. The day was pressing in on him heavily, and his decisions were haunting him. How did you ever know if you'd made the right ones?

He hadn't lied to Cecile about the boy, not really. He just hadn't told her everything he'd seen or heard that day. All he had wanted to do was give Marl a few days' breathing space, before letting Cecile worry. Now Carleton wondered if he should have let her worry, just a little bit.

With ten boys to watch over, you couldn't know everything that went on, but Carleton saw a great deal. He'd watched the boys in the potato garden from the kitchen window. He didn't have to hear a word to understand Topo's anger, and he hadn't missed Marl's frightened grip on the hoe. All the warning signals had flashed in the Englishman's head, but before he'd had a chance to move Goat was there. That surprised Carleton. He'd never known Goat to help anyone before.

But Goat hadn't been around for Marl's run-in with Len. Carleton remembered the blazing almond eyes. He wondered if anything could have averted that fight. The pale man leaned back and smoothed his thin copper-colored hair. One near fight and one actual explosion. Marl's "honeymoon" was over.

The boy's file sat on the desk in front of Carleton, piled as thick as an overstuffed mattress. Shoplifting, fighting, running away. He hadn't lasted in a single foster home for more than three months and he'd been in and out of Ryerson since he was eight. It was no wonder Cecile didn't know what to do anymore. Carleton remembered when she'd called.

"I . . . I'm at the end of the line with him, Carl." Her voice was brittle, sharp as the cutting edge of a tin can. "This is a one-shot deal. He goes back to Ryerson and it's closed custody for three years, no buts."

She inhaled, looking for the right words. "He's not bad, I mean, he's not cruel. He's just . . . restless. It doesn't say that in his file but . . . " She was stumbling, trying to explain something that was only a gut feeling. Carleton thought he understood.

"Bring him 'round," he had soothed. "Let's see what can be done." He'd been so hopeful then.

Now Carleton was pacing his study. He knew so little about the real Marl that he didn't know where to begin. The boy seemed distant, but did that mean that he couldn't be reached at all?

"Instinct," Carleton murmured thoughtfully. He had to trust his instinct. That worked for him sometimes, following his hunches. A hunch had told him not to mention what he'd seen in the garden, and one whispered something to him now. He glanced up at the ceiling.

"He might be asleep," he said aloud, but he knew it wasn't so. His instinct told him just what might help the boy with the almond eyes.

With neat, quick steps Carleton strode out of his study and lightly pattered up the stairs to the second floor, creaking only on the first step.

Goat sat on the edge of his bed in his pajamas, staring moodily at his fingernails. It was just June but the room was hot and the air hung heavily over the beds, even though the window was open. Carleton hadn't turned on the light. He listened at the door to the deep, rhythmic breathing of Topo and Cal, who shared the room with Goat. Hard work and fresh air made most of the boy heavy sleepers. Carleton felt quite sure that what he had come to say would not be overheard.

The tall fair man sat in a chair by the breezeless window, his shirt sticking to his back. Even in the heat Goat wore pajamas, the collar of the top buttoned as high as it would go. It almost hurt the Englishman to look at the boy, whose shoulder blades and collarbone poked up like sticks under a blanket. It wasn't that Goat was starving — he couldn't be — but he had a leathered leanness that reminded Carleton of someone who'd been out in the desert a long, long time.

"Well, laddie, what do you think of my idea?" Carleton asked quietly at last, when Goat hadn't responded.

The boy shrugged. "I kinda like being alone, y'know? I mean, I got nothing against the kid, I'm just used to being on my own."

Carleton nodded slightly. Even on his farm full of loners, Goat was the one apart. It was different from being aloof, or even shy. Goat simply lived entirely inside himself and had since he arrived at the farm. Still, Carleton had to try.

"You certainly helped the lad out today," he said.

"What?" Goat looked up, startled. He hadn't wanted anyone to see him out in the garden with the new kid. Goat didn't get involved in things like that, that wasn't him at all! He flushed with a sudden heat and sighed.

"I . . . I just didn't want to see him get beat up. He's not very big."

"It was a good thing you did," Carleton said. Goat grimaced but the Englishman continued on quickly.

"You're older, lad; the others look up to you. I think you could help Marl a great deal just be being there. Be his mate, like."

Goat lowered his eyes and bit the inside of his lip.

"In any event, you don't have to tell me now," Carleton said. "Only think about it, please?"

Goat shrugged again but Carleton stood up with a smile.

"There's a good lad, just think about it." He reached out to give the bony shoulder a squeeze, but Goat shrank back. Carleton was not surprised. He understood people who did not like to be touched.

When the man had left and the room was still, Goat flopped back, the bedsprings squeaking in disapproval.

Why? the boy wondered tiredly. Why, why me?

He didn't need the hassle, he didn't want to be somebody's "mate." All he wanted to do was survive until he was sixteen, and then maybe they'd let him go on his own. If he could stay out of trouble until then, maybe they'd let him go back into the world and he could be absorbed, lost in the crowd. He could find a place where he wouldn't be reminded every day that he was marked, and why.

The weight was heavy on Goat, pressing on his shoulders, his ribs. He closed his eyes and didn't even try to move.

There was a problem with Marl, Goat knew. Looking at him and hearing him talk was like being dragged back to where he himself had been three years ago. It was a place he never wanted to be again. Goat had heard that Marl ran away a lot. He understood that. He knew what it was like to have days that were full of holes where something should have been, and wasn't. He knew what it was like to live with a rage that was bigger than anything you could hold inside. He'd barely spoken to the boy with the funny eyes and still he felt he knew him, inside out. Goat didn't want to know anyone that well. He'd tell Carleton the next day that he'd have to find another mate for Marl.

The next morning Goat slept in, and he didn't get the chance to talk to the Englishman alone. By the end of the day, it was far, far too late.

4

"I say it's a capital idea," Carleton Jenner beamed brightly, "capital!"

The kitchen was warm and sunny, and the heat hadn't become stifling yet. Marl inhaled and the buttery smell of homemade waffles was comforting.

Carleton stabbed at the air with his fork for emphasis.

"A natural wonder," he said, "an invaluable source of education, not twenty minutes from here, and seven of you haven't seen it yet. That's a tragedy," he added gravely. "I could never forgive myself for not taking you."

Some of the boys slunk down in their chairs. The others concentrated on eating, watching only the waffles that Vilda slid onto their plates. No one wanted to go.

"Marl!" Carleton exclaimed and Marl jumped, the way he always did when someone actually said his name. "You'd like to go, wouldn't you? Imagine, actual dinosaur bones, a glimpse into life millions of years ago. We'd see the excavation sites and the canyons, layered with the sands of time."

Someone giggled and Len rolled his eyes but the Englishman ignored them.

"We could tour the museum," he continued excitedly. "It's fascinating. Wouldn't you like to go?"

Marl speared a sausage and began biting off chunks. Even if he'd wanted to go, he wouldn't have let Carleton know. Marl hadn't forgotten how the man had embarrassed him the evening before, in front of Len. He'd been sent to his room as if he were six years old. No, Marl thought, he wasn't going to help Carleton with his dumb plan.

"Well, it's settled then," the Englishman announced when Marl hadn't said anything. "We'll take the bus into town and see the museum. Then we'll continue on to Horsethief Canyon to view the Badlands at their finest. Marl," he said, pointing, "you go rouse Goat. Vilda dear, you'll come with us too."

"What?" she gasped, turning to stare as if Carleton had asked her to the moon.

"How come Goat got to sleep in?" Len asked pointedly. "*We* always have to get up."

"Ten boys to one adult?" Carleton asked the cook. "Family Services would murder me!" To Len he said, "It's my fault, I kept the lad up late last night."

"I *know,*" Topo said, a strange edge in his voice. Carleton caught it and became uneasy, but no one asked Topo how he knew.

"I'm only paid t'cook," Vilda grumbled, swabbing up the batter from the counters. "I'm not a babysitter. I've had my children, I don't have to suffer anymore."

"Marl," Carleton asked again, "please? Today?"

With a sigh, Marl pushed himself away from the table and trudged up the stairs. He turned into the room Goat shared with the others and glanced over the roughly made beds. Suddenly he sucked in his breath, as if someone had elbowed him in the stomach.

He couldn't have known that Goat always slept like that, his arms thrown over his head as if to protect himself. Marl felt as if he'd walked into someone's private hurt, an intruder in someone else's private space. He wanted to back up quickly, run out of the room, hide.

But pity held him there. Goat suddenly looked small and frightened, even though Marl couldn't see his face.

It was a shock to see someone who seemed as tough as a rusty nail look so thin and vulnerable.

A minute passed. What was he going to do? Standing there, the boy with the almond eyes felt awkward and embarrassed. He didn't want to get any closer. But what would he tell Carleton? That he had left Goat alone because he looked . . . sad?

Marl turned to his right and snatched a pillow off the rumpled bed. Squinting for accuracy, he aimed and threw.

Goat was jolted awake instantly. "What the? . . ."

Marl turned on his heel and fled through the door.

"Jenner said to get up," he called over his shoulder. Once he was out of sight, he leapt down the stairs two at a time.

". . . anyhow, the school up and tells my parents that I'm, y'know, a bad influence," Rayo was saying, "but I figure they just got something against Indians, 'cause I never did nothing myself. They didn't have any choice but to send me here, Mom and Dad. They're trying to get back on the reserve, y'know?"

Carleton Jenner's dirty white Volkswagen bus was bounding down the grid road on its way to the highway, and Rayo had plopped himself down in the seat next to Marl. He was a tall, amiable kid with a goofy smile and a body shaped like a fish: wider across the middle with large feet that stuck out like fins. Words came easily to Rayo and they left him easily too, like water pouring out of a watering can.

He was telling Marl his life's story and about how his family was kicked off the reserve.

"And they're full-blooded Cree, too," he said.

Marl looked sideways at Rayo whose hair was more brown than black and whose skin just looked deeply tanned.

"Well, we're *mostly* Cree," he explained. "There might be some other blood in there, but not much. Not enough to get kicked off a reserve for."

Marl never felt comfortable when people got close to

28

him and he wedged himself against the window. He wished Rayo would just shut up.

At the front of the bus, Vilda was praying.

"Dear Lord," she exclaimed as the bus slammed over each new bump. "Dear God!"

Her kinky black hair was flapping in the wind from the open windows and all the dust was making her sneeze.

"Atchoo!" Vilda's sneeze was followed by a gasp. "Dear God," she sniffled, her white knuckles wrapped around the bar in front of her seat.

Carleton Jenner was having a grand time. Grinning broadly, he hung one arm out the window to point out things he thought were of interest. The roar of the engine drowned him out completely. Even as the bus turned onto the smooth highway, Vilda was the only one who could hear him, and she didn't care about the scenery. She'd lived in the Badlands her whole life.

The highway into town twisted like a snake. Carleton slowed the dirty white bus to a crawl as it wound its way into the valley. The town was known as the Drum, and it desperately wanted to be a city. It wanted to be a city of bustling traffic and shiny new shopping centers, a city where young couples came to raise their families. The Drum wanted to be a place where things *happened*, and it wasn't.

Coal had once kept the town alive but the refinery was quiet now, its blackened stacks the only reminder of what had been. The Drum was dusty, its people shy. All they could offer was unusual scenery and the bones of creatures that had died out millions of years ago. That was enough to attract people, though. Scientists came to sift through the dirt, looking for fossils. Campers came to relax in the trailer park, photograph the splended canyons, and buy plastic dinosaurs for their children. The townspeople were proud of their archaeological treasures, less proud of the plastic dinosaurs.

"Damn!" Rayo breathed excitedly. "Willya look at that?"

Rayo had lived only in towns smaller than the Drum,

so the only scenery he knew was the flat prairie and the distant foothills. He leaned so close to the window that Marl could smell him—waffles and chocolate. Probably still sticky too. The boy with the long-drawn eyes turned them away to stare out the window.

The steep hills that banked the road looked sandy. Water had carved deep rivulets in them and smoothed away any sharp edges. The hills reminded Marl of half-melted blobs of ice cream. But ice cream didn't come in these colors! Shades of gray, green, brown, white, and rust were piled in layers. Marl never knew that dirt could look like that. Descending into the town, he felt a rush of excitement, as if they were entering another world. He would sooner have bitten his tongue than tell anyone, though.

"A thousand years," Carleton was announcing, "it took each layer a thousand years to form. You see, the raging river that created these hills brought with it the sediment of the ages . . ."

Like a happy tour guide, the Englishman chortled on until the Volkswagen bus pulled onto the main street of the Drum.

To someone like Marl, who'd lived his whole life in a *real* city, a booming, busy, humming city, it was deathly dull. The streets, the houses, the puny shopping center all seemed tattered and old. The museum didn't excite him either. What they saw weren't even the real bones. Plaster casts had been made and the originals were locked away in a safe, Carleton had told them. So what was the big deal then? Marl wondered.

It's dumb, he thought stubbornly. It just proved that nothing was ever what they said it would be. Not the homes they put you in, not the stupid bones they dragged you out to see.

The bus stopped at a traffic light and on Marl's side, there was a 7-11. Kids flowed in and out of the store. Some sat on their bikes in the parking lot, drinking Slurpees. The sun gleamed on them and one girl had her blonde hair tied back with a pink ribbon. She sucked up some slush through her straw, tried to spray it at another girl, and missed.

"Janet!" the other girl whined. "I'm telling Mom . . ."

Janet giggled and aimed again. It was summer, they were free. They were a whole different planet from Marl. He looked away.

His insides felt stretched as taut as a guitar string. He was edgy and his toes tapped to a nameless tune that was running around in his head. Cecile said that Marl had a problem with his feet—itchy feet, she called them. They took Marl places even when he knew he shouldn't go. Marl was good, just his feet were bad. As the bus headed out of town towards Horsethief Canyon, the nervous energy mounted inside him, like building blocks stacked one on another in a single teetering line to the sky.

"C'mon," Rayo urged in a hushed voice, "it'll be a blast."

The whispering was behind Marl, around the side of the bus. Half the troop was with Carleton, staring into the Badlands valley that everyone was already tired of. The boy with the almond eyes was sitting on the front bumper of the bus and his ears strained to hear more clearly.

He heard someone spit.

"What's the matter, chicken? Turning into a wimp?" The voice was slick and smug. It had to be Len.

"Look, what makes you think I can even drive?"

"Sh! Sh!"

They were so loud Marl expected Carleton and the others to turn around, but they didn't. The whispers began again in renewed secrecy.

"I *know* you can drive because I saw Jenner teach you," Len said.

"Yeah," piped up a young boy named Pete, "in case of an emergency or something. He had you practising out in the field for a whole week."

Rayo giggled as he spoke. He was itching for some action.

"C'mon," he coaxed again, "Jenner won't do anything. It'll be fun. We won't catch . . ."

The words froze in his throat as Marl turned the corner and they noticed him for the first time. His expression told them that his eyes might be funny, but his ears worked just fine.

Goat, who was leaning against the side of the bus, stared at his runners. He didn't have to look up. He knew who it was.

Like some flippin' shadow, he thought to himself. The kid shows up everywhere!

The boy with the scarred face was suddenly angry, remembering what Jenner had asked him to do. What did Jenner think he was, some kind of baby-sitter? The more he thought about it, the angrier he became. Jenner wasn't his social worker, he couldn't tell Goat what to do or who to hang around with. He gave a rock a vicious kick and it bounded over the tufts of grass.

"Let's go for it," he muttered. Pete gave an excited jump and Rayo elbowed him to keep quiet.

Len was watching Marl, a hard, half smile fixed on his face.

"Well, suck," he asked, "you coming or ya gonna squeal to Jenner?"

Len's voice prodded Marl like a sharp stick. He clenched his hands tight, tighter. Len was responsible for the big mess the night before, he was the reason Marl had been sent to his room. All the bad feelings were still there, balled up in a desperate angry *something* that was tearing at Marl's insides. It was Carleton's fault, too. The Englishman had betrayed him, treated him like a baby.

"He deserves this," Marl thought darkly. Carleton Jenner deserved to have his day ruined. What did they care anyway? They were already ruined kids.

"I'll come," Marl said.

Stealthily, Rayo peered around the edge of the bus.

"It's okay," he whispered. "He's busy giving one of his speeches."

The mud-splattered side door of the bus slid open easily and the boys slipped in, unnoticed. When the bus had first stopped at the canyon, the boys had seen Carleton put the keys into his jacket pocket. A few minutes later, the Englishman had returned the jacket to the bus, complaining about the heat. Now Goat crept to the driver's seat where the jacket lay and fumbled through the pockets. In a moment the keys were tinkling in his hand.

Near the edge of the cliff a hundred meters away, Carleton was explaining to his dull-eyed audience how Horsethief Canyon had acquired its name.

"Halfway through the 1800s," Carleton said with a flourish, "the ranchers in the valley began noticing that their horses were disappearing in the dark of the night. They assembled search parties and sometimes the animals were found wandering in the canyon, but their brand marks had been strangely altered. No one could prove . . ."

The first rumble of the Volkswagen engine cut Carleton short and he spun around.

"Good Lord!" Vilda gasped and the others stood open mouthed in disbelief.

Goat saw Carleton leap into a run and desperately he stomped on the clutch, pushing in the gearshift. The gears ground, screaming, but they wouldn't budge.

Goat swore and his foot kicked at the clutch again. This time, the bus slipped into first but when Goat stepped on the gas pedal, the engine jerked, choked, and died.

"For chrissakes, hurry!" Rayo screamed. Sweat was blinding Goat. He clenched his teeth and scrambled for the ignition.

Now that Carleton could see what they planned, he was frightened. Running full tilt he was closing the gap between himself and the bus: forty meters . . . thirty-five.

Goat rammed the gearshift into first once more and eased up on the clutch. The bus jerked forward and then began to move sluggishly as Goat pulled hard left on the steering wheel. Slowly it gathered speed and they swung out in a wide circle, heading for the road back into town. In his rearview mirror Goat saw Carleton standing helplessly on the grass where the bus had been, his arms limp at his sides. Goat grinned and pushed harder on the gas pedal. The bus shuddered as he shifted into second gear.

Rayo, Len, and Pete were hooting with triumph now, slamming one another on the shoulders, clapping Goat on the back.

"Back off and sit down," he growled, but they were too excited to listen.

"Did you *see* him?" Len cried. "Did you see the look on his face? He was like a little kid who got his bike stolen!"

"And there we were, just motorin' away," Rayo laughed.

Marl was sitting in one of the front seats, his feet in the aisle, grinning. He felt breathlessly free and brave. They could do anything, go anywhere! Shyly he glanced at the wiry arms and hands that handled the steering wheel. As soon as he could, Marl vowed he would find someone to teach him to drive too.

The bus was bounding over the rough trail and the boys who were standing kept banging into one another and laughing with glee. Pete was even thrown into Marl's lap with the lurching of the bus.

"Ow!" Marl cried, as an elbow flew into his rib cage.

"Sit down!" Goat barked over his shoulder. "Or I'll stop this flippin' bus right now."

He sounded serious, like somebody's parent, and the giddy air in the bus went flat. Just what was Goat trying to pull, Len wondered, his eyes hardening behind the gold rims.

I'm the one who thought this up, he said to himself. I should be the one making the rules.

But Goat was driving. Goat was the only one who could drive, Len knew that. So there was nothing for him to do but drop grudgingly into his seat with the others. For a moment the only sound was the chugging of the engine and the squeaking of the suspension.

"All right," Goat said at last, "you've got about forty-five minutes. Where do you want to go?"

"Forty-five minutes?" Rayo asked.

"It'll take half an hour for Jenner to walk into town and fifteen minutes for the cops to find us."

Pete sat up straight in his seat, suddenly looking very much his ten years of age.

"He wouldn't," he breathed. "Would he?"

One of Goat's gaping silences hung in the air. He didn't have to answer.

They were approaching the Drum and when Goat pulled up to the first stoplight, everyone tensed. The boys knew that a lot of underage kids drove in a town as small as the Drum: They were farm kids, used to driving tractors and trucks and not about to stop once they hit the city. Still, no one wanted to attract attention to the dirty white bus so they sat as quietly as statues, staring straight ahead.

The light turned green, but Goat had left the bus in third gear. It lurched forward, the engine crying in pain, and stalled dead. Everyone stiffened as Goat fumbled to start it again. They could feel the drivers behind them growing impatient.

Goat was muttering under his breath and his hands had begun to tremble. The longer it took, the more nervous he got, until his knees were shaking too. Finally, cars began pulling out around them, throwing angry side glances as they passed. Frantic now, Goat kept flicking the ignition but the Volkswagen was temperamental: The engine sputtered and wouldn't turn over.

"You were right," Len snapped. "You *can't* drive!"

Goat's raw nerves had been stretched too far. He whirled around, his gray-blue eyes stormy and wild.

"Shut your face, Len," he hissed, "or I'll shut it for you!"

Len flew to his feet, his sharp jaw thrust forward. In

35

one quick move he whipped off his glasses and stood there, challenging.

"You think so, punk?" he said. "C'mon, right now!"

Marl's sense of freedom had been jerked out from underneath him like a rug. Why did things always go bad when they were going good? They didn't have time for this, they didn't have time!

"For chrissakes, not here," he spat at them. "You," he said to Goat, "get this thing started and get us out of here. And you," he pointed at Len, "just sit down and shut up for once."

His voice carried strange authority. The words had weight. There was no denying that Marl was right and Len looked uncomfortably at the dark-eyed boy.

"That kid's getting to be a real pest," he thought, but the others seemed to agree with Marl. Len dropped into his seat with a thud, his arms folded over his chest.

Goat turned back to the wheel then, thankful that no one could see the relief in his face. The tension had blown over and his legs were steady now. He started the bus on his first try and shifted easily into second gear as the bus picked up speed.

Marl was trembling. He slumped into his seat, surprised that he had actually said something to them. He hadn't meant to but the anger had taken over.

Damn them, Marl thought. All everybody cared about was their own image, what they looked like to everybody else. It meant one squabble after another, days piled on days filled with nothing but fights. And in that moment Marl knew that he was very, very tired of it.

He closed his eyes and missed the surprised, grateful glance the driver gave him.

5

Goat was wrong about Carleton: The Englishman was faster than he thought. In just twenty minutes Carleton's long strides were pulling him into the Drum.

"Stay here!" he had called to Vilda. "Don't let anyone out of your sight, for anything!"

"Wait . . ." the cook cried, but Carleton was already on his way, fear moving his feet.

For a moment she just stood there, feeling helpless and angry.

I knew it! Vilda said to herself. I could have told him something like this would happen. We shouldn't have come, not in a hundred years!

A hot wind blew over the Badlands, burning her eyes and scorching her throat. She stared vacantly at the group that Carleton had left her to watch over. They were clustered over by the sign that said "Horsethief Canyon," buzzing with the news. The sign also said "screw" in large orange letters where it had been spray-painted over the official notice. That irked Vilda, irritated her more than she already was.

Kids, she thought. They probably did that. No respect for anybody else, ruining what isn't theirs just because it isn't.

In this mood, she curled her hands into fists and rested them on her hips.

"All right," she called loudly, "everybody back, back where I can see you!"

Grumbling, they drifted over to where she stood, their hands dug deep into their pocket, their eyes squinting in the Badlands sun.

"We weren't doin' nothing," the curly haired boy named Cal said. "You people, you're always hassling us, for no reason,"

"Hmph!" Vilda muttered. "That's why you're all here, caught doing nothing, I suppose?"

"Yeah, you got it," Cal said, his chin jutting out. "They stuck us here because they didn't want to look after us. Ain't that right, Tope?"

Topo was surly. No one had asked *him* if he wanted to go along for the ride. He remembered the night before, all the words he'd heard while lying in the dark, pretending to sleep. No one had ever tried to find a friend for *him*.

They're all against me, Topo thought. Nobody cares. I gotta fight for everything I get. These feelings settled in his stomach, heavy and gritty as sand.

"Yeah, that's right," Topo answered Cal at last. A thick lock of chestnut-red hair fell across his eyes. "I never did nothing, either."

The brilliant orange "screw" on the sign seemed to catch in Vilda's eye, hurting like a grain of sand. It pushed her further than she would ever have gone otherwise.

"You never did nothing?" she repeated. "You wouldn't have gone with those . . . hoodlums if you had the chance?"

Topo's shoulders tensed. How could she have known what he was thinking? Vilda heard his silence and felt herself growing large and powerful. She didn't want that but she couldn't stop it.

"Sure, you would have gone," she snapped. "You're all the same. One's not better than the other. Ungrateful hoodlums, stealing a bus!"

Her accusation prodded Topo, pushed him out of his silence.

"And what have we got to be grateful for?" he asked. "Tell me that, huh?"

"You've got the clothes on your back, a roof to sleep under, and three meals a day," Vilda rattled off. "That's more than a lotta people got."

"So what?" Topo sneered, moving in, warming up. "It's not our fault we're here. If our parents had been half-decent, we wouldn't be like we are."

He saw in her face that he'd struck a nerve; Vilda paled and her jaw tightened. He had her now. He wouldn't give up.

"You're the ones who brought us into this screwed-up world of yours," he continued, "and then when you can't handle it, you just dump us off on somebody else. Or maybe we know we're not wanted and we take off. Who wouldn't run away from somebody like you?"

There was a pause, a heartbeat. "Don't you dump that 'grateful' shit on me, lady," Topo said finally. "I'm not takin' any blame. I didn't ask to be born."

"And we'd be better off if you never were!" Vilda breathed suddenly, in pain.

Topo flinched as if he'd been stabbed. Grown-ups weren't supposed to say things like that. All the social workers and court people and foster parents Topo knew didn't say things like that. He opened his mouth but no words came out. When he tried to swallow his throat hurt. He could only stare at Vilda with wet, open eyes.

The cook had deflated; she felt suddenly small. She'd gone too far, oh, too far! The half-grown man in front of her was suddenly only a young, wounded boy. She hadn't meant to do that!

But she couldn't apologize. All the boys were standing there, staring at her. She couldn't admit she was wrong in front of the children. They had already seen her flustered and angry. Adults weren't supposed to be like that. They were supposed to be in control, and right, all the time.

Vilda turned away, hating where she was, hating why

she was there. In the corner of her eye she could still see the glowing orange "screw," laughing and laughing as it swung in the wind.

Carleton Jenner leaned forward in the squad car, his pianist's fingers clutching the seat in front of him between the two officers. He desperately wanted them to see things his way.

"They're not really *bad*," he said. "They're just high-spirited lads."

"Who steal buses," Officer Rowan remarked, shoulder checking as he pulled out of the police station parking lot. He was a heavyset man with wide shoulders and a square jaw; his dark hair was cut high above the collar. Everything about him was big: his hands, his powerful arms. He had the rounded, smooth movements of a bear, but Dan Rowan was more graceful than any bear could be.

Officer Bleans sat half turned in his seat, scribbling notes on his pad. With his strawberry hair and bright blue eyes, he looked not much older than some of the boys who came to the Jenner farm. In truth he was just twenty, and only six months out of the Calgary Police Academy.

Take notes, they had instructed Jeffery Bleans there, and the young man had become a note-taker after Carleton's own heart.

"Can you give me the names and ages of the suspects once more, Mr. Jenner?" Officer Bleans asked politely.

Carleton winced at the word "suspects."

"They're not really criminals," he said again, "just . . ."

"High-spirited," Officer Rown supplied.

"Yes!" Carleton said, not catching the edge in the policeman's voice. Jefferey Bleans was waiting patiently, his pen poised.

"Oh," the Englishman said, recalling Officer Bleans's request, and placed his fingers over his mouth, remembering. "There's Len Powell, he's thirteen; and little Pete Zamoyski, ten. Rayo Johnsguard is also thirteen, Marl Silversides is twelve, and Goat is fourteen."

"Goat?" Officer Bleans asked.

"Oh . . . uh, Greg Land. Goat is his nickname," Carleton explained.

"I take it this Goat is the driver?" Officer Rowan said, his eyes never leaving the road.

"Yes," Carleton said softly, "I taught him to drive myself. In the event of an emergency, you understand. I thought it would be good for him."

He looked directly into the blue, blue eyes of Officer Bleans.

"These boys need so much," Carleton said. "They've had bad starts, or maybe bad middles. You don't always know what will work with them, or if anything ever will, but you have to keep trying."

Jeffery Bleans had stopped taking notes; he was listening too hard. Fourteen was not so long ago for him.

"You may not believe me," Carleton said, "but no matter where these boys have been or what they've done, I think there's something . . . truly good . . . in each one of them."

For a moment, no one spoke. The only sound was the police radio, rambling quietly in the background. Finally Officer Rowan leaned forward and squinted.

"White Volkswagen bus?" he asked, and rattled off the license number.

"Yes, yes, it's them," Carleton breathed, relieved and nervous at the same time. "Please, no siren," he asked as Officer Rowan reached to turn it on; "we don't want to scare them into the ditch. I only said he could drive, I never said he was good at it."

Dan Rowan shrugged his great bear shoulders and stepped on the accelerator.

Rayo was the first to spot the police cruiser.

"Damnit, Goat," he hissed, "it's the cops!"

Goat's hands clenched the steering wheel and a shudder went through his body. His eyes leapt to the rearview mirror.

"Sure is," he said grimly; "the ride's over."

Len lunged to the front seat of the bus. "C'mon, go for it," he cried, shoving Goat on the shoulder. "Don't give up yet. We'll give 'em a chase, just for the hell of it."

Goat, who did not like being touched at the best of times, wrenched his shoulder away and glared at Len.

"It's over," he insisted.

"Don't be such a suckhole," Len sneered. "First you don't even want to go, and now you're ready to pack it in. Yeah, I heard about you. They guys at Ryerson said you were a ____"

"They're getting closer!" Pete called from the back of the bus. "They're pullin' up beside us."

"See!" Len said, shoving Goat again. "C'mon, move it, or let me drive."

"BACK OFF!" Goat was furious now. With his right hand he swung at Len and missed, pulling on the steering wheel to balance himself. The Volkswagen swerved and Marl gasped, clutching at the dashboard in front of him.

Officer Rowan, who had just pulled up beside them, swerved too, blasting his horn to warn other drivers.

"My God!" Carleton cried. "They'll crash!"

But somehow, the bus centered in its lane again and Officer Rowan sped up until the cruiser was exactly alongside the driver's door. Jeffery Bleans leaned out his window with a bull horn.

"Greg Land," his young voice boomed, "pull this vehicle over."

The noise was blaring and distorted. "What?" Goat said, thrusting his head out the window.

"Pull over," Jeffery Bleans cried again. "Pull over!"

Goat did precisely as he was told, too fast and too soon. The bus swung crazily into a one hundred and eighty degree turn before screeching to a stop at the side of the road, one wheel in the ditch.

Dan Rowan was there first, flinging open the front passenger door with one easy pull of his powerful arm.

"Are you hurt, boy?" he asked. Marl shook his head

numbly. He was staring at the policeman who looked ten feet tall.

As easily as he would pick up a rag doll, the bear-man lifted Marl out of his seat and stood him on the ground next to the bus. He unlatched the side door of the bus and slid it open quickly, asking each of the boys if he was all right and helping them outside. Pete started to whine in the back of his throat and Marl wasn't surprised. *His* insides felt like jello too. He leaned against the bus for support.

Officer Bleans was in the police car, radioing in the call, and Carleton simply stood, staring at them. He didn't know whether to be relieved or furious.

With one huge hand on Pete's shoulder, Officer Rowan steered him out of the bus. In a moment of emotion, the Englishman flung his arms around Pete, squeezing so hard that the boy gasped. Then he pulled back, clutching Pete's shoulders.

"I could just murder you!" Carleton said. "The scare you lads gave me. You should all be whipped."

Dan Rowan rested his hands on his hips, on his gun belt.

"Well, nobody seems to be hurt," he said in his slow, steady way. "Will you be wanting to press charges, Mr. Jenner?"

Carleton stood up, looking blank.

"Charges?" he asked.

Officer Bleans had finished his call to the police station and he was staring too. He had never been through anything like this. What would his partner do?

"To tell the truth, Mr. Jenner, this is grand theft auto, an indictable offense. Even though the boys are minors . . ." Officer Rowan's voice trailed off; he saw Pete pale.

"Oh," Carleton said, dismayed, "is there really a need? I . . . I will be making a report, to Family Services and the boys' social workers. I assure you, this incident won't go unpunished."

Jeffery Bleans was staring intently, his lips parted. He wanted to jump in, say something, tell Dan to let it go. He didn't know that Dan Rowan was one step ahead of him. Small town constables had to use their own judgment sometimes, and this time the officer just wanted to make an impression on the boys.

"Well, I guess we could let it go with a warning," Officer Rowan said at last, "but I'd like to check back with you, to see what steps are being taken. It's my responsibility to protect this town," he added, looking directly at Goat.

The boy with the spiky blonde hair leaned to his left and spat.

Carleton was still too shaken to drive so it was agreed that Officer Rowan would take the bus up to Horsethief Canyon to pick up Vilda and the others. Jeffery Bleans waited shyly with Carleton's crew, sitting with the door of the cruiser open, his feet on the grass. He wanted to help but he didn't know how.

Now that the moments of panic were over, the Englishman was feeling angry and hurt. All he'd wanted to do was give the boys a good day. He had trusted them and they had let him down.

He stood, searching their faces, his mouth drawn into a thin line. Marl knew that look, he'd seen it before. It was an I'm-going-to-get-to-the-bottom-of-this! kind of stare that Marl dreaded. Leaning against the back end of the police car, he turned his head sideways and stared off down the road.

I'm not saying nothin', Marl thought. I'm just gonna keep my mouth shut and let it all blow over. Maybe if he was quiet they wouldn't notice him, would forget that he was involved at all. The boy with the almond eyes knew you had to watch out for yourself.

"I want to know and I want to know *now*," Carleton said stiffly, "whose bright idea was this?"

"It was Goat's!" Len piped up suddenly, slipping into a little-boy voice. "He said he'd kick our teeth in if we didn't go."

"I did not," Goat shot back but Rayo cut him off.

"Yeah, it was Goat," the almost-Cree boy agreed quickly. He didn't dislike Goat, but it was every man for himself. "He said you wouldn't care . . ."

Marl felt a jab in his stomach, as if something had twisted.

Don't, he warned himself, but he felt funny. He tried not to hear but he couldn't turn off his ears.

Pete sniffled for dramatic effect. "It was Goat," he whined, and he let a sob rise in his throat. "He's always tellin' us what to do."

Marl couldn't stand it.

"It was us!" he blurted out, "All of us. We all decided. It wasn't just one person."

Carleton looked into one face and then another.

"Well, then I'm holding you all responsible. You *all* should have known better!"

Len glared at Marl, the sun glinting on the gold rims of his glasses, but the doe-skinned boy wasn't watching, Head down, he was studying his sneakers, trying to become invisible.

When things went bad, they went real bad, Marl was thinking. Oh, why did he even go with them in the first place? Jenner would tell Cecile and Cecile would tell Family Services. They'd ship him back to Ryerson on the next bus.

What if Cecile gave up on him for real this time? He would have nobody then. What did you do when you wanted to be good but only chances to be bad came up? It didn't matter what he did, Marl thought numbly. He already knew how things would turn out.

Officer Rowan soon arrived with Vilda's half of the group who were strangely quiet. Marl didn't look up but he could feel their eyes, staring curiously through the windows of the bus. Why did people have to look at you just when you wanted to disappear? The July heat hung in the valley but Marl felt cold.

With half an ear, he listened as Carleton thanked the

45

policemen, apologized, and then thanked them again. Like all grown-ups, they stood around talking long after they should have said goodbye.

"Hey," a quiet voice in front of him said suddenly. "Hey . . . Marl."

Marl raised his head and squinted through his long eyelashes; the sun was harshly bright.

"Yeah, what?" he asked.

Goat's hands were buried in his pockets and he stared at his feet, which scuffed nervously at the dirt.

"I'd like to, uh, say thanks," Goat said quickly, "for today, for everything."

Marl was stunned. He had never expected anything like this, nor would he have imagined it. He was embarrassed. What did you say to something like that?

"It wasn't anything," Marl began but Goat cut him off.

"Yeah," the other boy nodded, "yeah, it *was* something. You didn't have to stick up for me. I mean, I never would have asked you to." He paused. "You know, when you first came here, I thought you were a dumb kid, but really, you're okay."

He looked into Marl's eyes then, and a grin twisted half his face. To Marl's surprise, he found himself grinning back —he couldn't help it. A warm feeling was spreading through his chest. It was like finding a Christmas present with your name on it, or being picked first for a soccer team.

"You're okay," Marl whispered to himself after Goat had moved on, and he liked the sound of it in his ear.

"Everyone in!" Carleton called, and the last few boys hurried through the side door of the bus. Just before he followed them in, Marl noticed a piece of a broken stick lying on the grass. He snatched it up and hid it in his hand so no one could see.

You just didn't have too many good days, Marl thought, and when you did, you didn't get to keep them forever. He wanted to save this one somehow, if only for a little while. Marl held onto the stick all the way home, until it was so warm it felt like part of his hand.

6

_____

"We gotta _what_?" Len asked, his hands on his hips. It was the next day and Carleton had the five boys in the kitchen for a "chat" right after lunch. He hadn't seen any of them until now: He'd spent the whole morning on the phone.

"Well, you have a choice," Carleton said. "You can spend two weeks under house arrest or you can clean the bus."

"What's house arrest?" Pete asked.

"Just what it sounds like," the Englishman said crisply. "No leaving the house, no T.V., no treats. You'll do your chores and spend the rest of the time in your rooms."

Their blank faces were horrified. "Or you can clean the bus," Carleton continued, "and I mean spic and span. Vacuum, polish, inside and out. I'd rent an upholstery cleaner for the seats."

"No way," Rayo said, his voice wide with disbelief, "not the seats too."

"The seats too." Carleton was firm. "At the rate of fifty cents an hour it should take approximately six hours to pay back what expenses you incurred for gas and wear and tear."

Rayo groaned and Marl sighed, but Len was smiling his superior smile.

"Hey, don't worry about it," he told the others. "It's not fair. He can't make decisions like this. Our workers won't let him. We don't have to do any of it."

Carleton's voice fell like a stone. "Oh, yes you will, laddie. Your workers have already agreed. They think my choices are very fair."

"Not Jim," Len said defiantly. "Jim wouldn't go for it."

"Jim *especially* thought it was an admirable idea," Carleton answered evenly. He would never let the boy know how much wheedling it had taken to convince the new social worker.

"I'll take the house thing," Pete said sullenly but Rayo elbowed him and Carleton shook his head.

"You *all* have to agree. Now, what will it be? Two weeks of house arrest or a day of work?"

There was a heavy pause and another sigh. "We'll do the damn bus," Len muttered.

"All right, you can start right away. You'll need soap and water and some rags. There's chrome polish underneath the sink."

The boys stood there, eyeing him narrowly.

"Well, hop to it," the Englishman cried, clapping his hands. "The sooner you get started the sooner you'll finish." The boys began moving wearily, swearing under their breath.

Just as Carleton was heading towards the door, Marl took an uncertain step forward.

Carleton paused. "Yes, Marl?"

The boy's hands were scrunched up in his pockets and he flicked his head so that his long bangs were out of his eyes for a moment.

"Did . . . did you talk to Cecile too?"

When the man nodded Marl asked, "What did she say?"

"She said she'd like to talk to you when she came down, before her holidays."

"Was she mad?"

"She was disappointed," Carleton replied honestly, searching the brown almond eyes. He wondered if the boy knew how exotic they looked.

Marl was nodding to himself, as if he'd heard what he'd expected to hear. "Yeah, okay," he said, sauntering away behind the pack of boys. Then, as if he suddenly remembered, he turned and said, "Thanks."

Carleton could not hide his smile. Marl was actually being polite.

"You're welcome," the Englishman murmured, and he watched for a moment as Marl walked away, wondering what was going on under the dark, thick curtain of hair.

"This isn't so bad," Marl was thinking. He could have been sent back to Ryerson or charged by the police. Cleaning a bus didn't seem so terrible.

He was wrong. The sun was hard, hard as the heel of a boot, and it squashed the boys who worked under it. It seemed to pin them to the ground: Marl felt he could barely move. No one had told him about the Badlands in July.

It was because of the heat that Carleton relented a bit. Marl, Pete, Rayo, Len, and Goat were freed from their other chores that day. They just had to finish the bus. Just, Marl thought. Carleton kept bringing out pitchers of icewater but the boys felt as slow and sticky as pancake syrup.

Marl had been given the job of polishing the bus with paste wax, and it was the hardest work he could ever remember doing. It even beat hoeing the potato garden. First he had to smear the paste onto a small patch of the clean exterior of the bus with a cloth, and wait for it to dry. In the hot sun that happened quickly, barely giving Marl a break. Then he had to take another cloth and rub the patch until the paste was gone and the paint shone. After half an hour Marl had left a streaky three-foot trail that looked worse than the dirt. He slumped to the ground, exhausted.

Carleton's heart was softening like butter under the Badlands sun. By two o'clock he was speaking gently to everyone and even brought out cookies, although it was just after lunch. When he saw Marl sitting so dejectedly against the bus he was drawn over, as if by a magnet.

"Tough job, isn't it, laddie?" the Englishman asked.

"Yeah," Marl admitted, preparing himself for a lecture, but none came.

"I think I'll send you over some help then," Carleton said, looking at Marl's streak that ended just below the windows of the bus. "Someone who can hit the high spots."

When Goat appeared, squinting in the glare, Marl was not surprised. Carleton seemed to put them on a lot of chores together.

Goat was staring at the area that Marl had polished, shaking his head. He leaned to his left and spit.

"Boy, you've never done this before, have you?" Goat said.

"Oh sure," Marl said, pulling himself to his feet, "lots of times."

Goat leaned down and picked up the soft cotton rag that Marl was supposed to buff with. He leaned on the spot and rubbed it hard, really moving his arms, knowing that Marl was watching. When he had finished, panting and hot, he said, "C'mere and see."

Marl peered at the spot which was now so shiny he could see his face in it. He blinked and turned away.

"Oh," he said.

"Here," Goat tossed the cloth, "you do it now, and really rub."

Marl attacked another streaky patch and tried to move his arms as quickly and powerfully as Goat had. He was thinking about those arms, how they didn't look like there was anything to them but were so solid and wiry underneath. Marl was gasping by the time he had finished, but his patch was just as shiny as the one Goat had done. The older boy gave him a good-natured nod.

"Yeah, great. Now I'll do one."

They took turns, one resting while the other polished, and Marl didn't feel nearly so tired as before, or as strangled by the heat. Something was bubbling inside him, humming like electricity through the great power lines he had seen.

"I went to this school once," Marl said suddenly, the energy bursting out of him, "and half of it was this high school."

"Oh yeah," Goat said.

"Well, they had an autobody shop for the grade tens and regular people would bring their cars in for the kids to work on and stuff. They took us on a tour once, to show us."

He paused for a moment, not sure whether Goat wanted to hear the story or not. The silence seemed to say that he did.

"Anyhow," Marl continued, "they used to polish all the cars they worked on, just like this. I guess it was so nobody could tell right away if they'd wrecked the car or fixed it."

Goat, who was smearing more paste onto the bus, stopped and cocked his head in disbelief. "No way, all they'd have to do is turn it over."

"Turn it upside down?" Marl asked and Goat laughed, actually laughed.

"No, dummy," he chuckled, "turn over the engine. You know, start the car?"

"Oh sure, I knew that," Marl said quickly. "I was just testing."

Goat shook out his rag with a snap! and turned his head slightly. The scar disappeared in the crease of a smile, a smile that told Marl he was funny, but okay.

Goat was a different kind of guy, Marl was thinking. With his gaunt, bony features and dark circles under his eyes, Goat looked like other kids Marl knew: tough kids, bitter kids. But that's where Goat was different. He seemed hard, but not angry. A shadow of sadness clung to the boy and it made Marl hungry to know more about him. Marl did not wonder about too many people.

"How long have you been here?" he asked.

"A year," Goat said and Marl couldn't tell if it had been a good year or a bad year.

"Where were you before that?"

"Oh, around," Goat said. "At Ryerson mostly."

"Me too," Marl answered. "I never saw you there."

Goat shrugged his shoulders, concentrating on the part of the bus that was under his rag. "I was kinda, uh, in closed custody some of the time."

"What for?"

"Fighting."

"What were you doing at Ryerson in the first place?" the dark-eyed boy wanted to know.

Goat's hands stopped moving and he leaned against his new shine, squinting suspiciously at Marl.

"You sure got a lot of questions, kid," he said.

Marl was thinking fast. "Yeah, I'm gonna be a cop when I grow up," he said lightly and Goat knew right away that he was kidding. A half grin crept its way onto the left side of Goat's face.

"Okay, officer," he said, moving back so that Marl could take his turn at the bus, "when I was eleven, I was with these guys and we got picked up for B and E."

Marl knew that "B and E" meant "breaking and entering" and he was properly impressed.

"At eleven?" he breathed.

Goat nodded. "I was small, I fit through windows better, especially basement windows. They'd jimmy one open and I'd slip in and then let them in through the front door, like they were friends coming to visit or something."

"Smart," Marl murmured, smearing a new circle of wax. Goat snorted in disgust and a bitter edge crinkled his voice.

"Yeah, it was real smart," he said. "It was so smart it only took 'em three weeks to catch us and slap us into Ryerson."

He was leaning his bony shoulder blades against the bus, staring at his thumbs which were hooked through the belt loops of his jeans.

"And I was so smart I beat the shit out of anybody who got in my way. All the time they were laughin', adding time to my sentence. And I didn't even care because I figured I could take care of myself."

He paused and Marl felt the heat of the day, pressing, pressing.

"But you can't, you can't beat 'em all." Goat was talking only for himself now, his voice sunk to a whisper. "And when it was over, nobody would even listen to my side of the story. They just stuck me in closed custody because they didn't know what else to do."

The weight was on Goat and he felt numb with tiredness, as if all the words had been only a dream. Marl stared. He knew he was seeing a kid that other people didn't see and hearing things no one else had been told. Marl had other questions but he didn't ask them. Goat looked breakable somehow, and young. Marl thought of how Goat slept, his head buried in his arms as if he were hiding from the night.

I know, Marl thought to himself, I know what that's like, what bad dreams are. Even when you think you got your days all together, the nights creep up and blow it for you.

Rousing himself, Goat noticed that Marl was staring at him and he looked away, embarrassed. He bent down to pick up another rag and sniffed, recovering.

"So anyhow, kid," said Goat, the old-timer, the one who knew, "you may think cleaning a bus is bad but it's nothing compared to C.C. at Ryerson."

"Okay, when I'm a cop you can clean the squad cars," Marl kidded. Goat looked quickly over his shoulder and suddenly flicked his rag, aiming for the back of Marl's jeans. Surprised, Marl blinked, and then he laughed. He twirled his own rag and snapped it at Goat, who dodged and took aim again. The friendly snap, snap! rang out over the prairie.

From the porch of the farmhouse, Topo couldn't make out what Marl and Goat were saying, but the sound of their voices clattered against him like pebbles thrown at a window. There was no mistaking the laughter, or the friendly war with the rags. If this was punishment, how come they were having such a good time? Topo remembered the night that Carleton had crept in to talk to Goat, and what he had asked him to do. The bitterness burned brightly in Topo's eye.

"Nobody," he thought, "nobody ever did that for me."

Topo rubbed his snub sun burnt nose with the back of his hand. It seemed to him that Marl's arrival had marked the beginning, the start of the slide from bad to worse. He thought about the trip into the Drum and the adventure no one had asked him to go on. They'd asked Marl, and he was just new. Everybody seemed to think the kid was just great, Topo grumbled. Nobody told Marl that he shouldn't have been born. The heavyset boy wouldn't let himself think about Vilda or what she'd said to him on the ridge of Horsethief Canyon. He only knew that something was gnawing at his insides, tiny razor-sharp teeth that wouldn't let him forgive or forget.

7

Disaster, Marl was beginning to realize, never happened when it was supposed to. It never came when you were ready for it. Catastrophes occurred when everything was quiet and you were thinking that the world wasn't such a bad place after all.

It was evening and most of the boys were in the rec room. Some were watching T.V. but Goat, Len, and Brucie were playing cards at a small table. Marl was watching them. He leaned against the side of the couch, a foot away from Brucie's left elbow. The game was blackjack and Len was dealing.

"You gotta pay to play," Len sang, snapping down the cards. Goat and Brucie tossed their wooden match sticks into the "pot" in the center of the table. The boys had no money, of course, but matches were useful. There was no telling when you might run across some cigarettes. Unwary social workers would frequently leave the farm after a visit, not missing the packet of cigarettes which had been taken from their pocket until they were on the highway once more, traveling back to the city.

"Shady lady," Len said, turning over the queen of spades for Brucie. "Hit or stay?"

Brucie lifted the edge of his face-down card. Marl saw that it was a two.

"Hit me," Brucie said. Len bent a card with his fingers

so that it shot forward, flying into Brucie's face. The boy giggled, grabbing for the card. He laid it on the table, bringing into view the eight of clubs.

"Eighteen up," Len said. "I bet you bust."

"Bust? Where's a bust?" Cal cried across the room. "I haven't seen a good pair in ages!"

Everybody laughed, even Marl. He was comfortable, listening to the chatter around the card table and watching Len play the dealer, as if he were in Las Vegas.

The whole day had been pretty good, Marl thought. Working on the bus with Goat, Marl felt for the first time that he wasn't in a detention home. He could almost pretend he was at camp or something, like a regular kid. He and Goat had done a really good job together; even Jenner had said so. The Englishman had scampered around the bus saying, "A genuine hand-rubbed shine! It's marvelous, absolutely marvelous!"

Even now, the words made Marl feel giddy. Nothing could bother him tonight, not Len, not the heat, not anything. He felt like part of the gang.

At the card table, Goat was betting high and losing good-naturedly. He had only four match sticks left, plus one that was clamped between his teeth. Laid on the table in front of him were a four and a six, as well as the face-down card.

"Stay or play?" Len asked, his hands poised to deal.

"Sure, what the hell," Goat said, pushing his matches into the pile. Len turned up the king of diamonds.

"Man with the ax," Len chortled, raking in the pot. "You got the ax all right!"

"Ah, who cares about matches," Goat said. He leaned back in his chair, hands clasped behind his neck. "Me and Marl are gonna be rich anyway."

"Oh, sure."

"How?"

"We're gonna have this business," Goat said, the match stick held tight in his grin, "polishing cars."

Everyone knew how the boys had spent their day and

they laughed. Marl groaned and fell back onto the couch. He didn't want anyone to see how delighted he was.

Smashing glass froze the laughter in the boys' throats. Their eyes turned up to stare at the ceiling. Above them, they heard muffled obscenities, rising sharply and falling. There were heavy footsteps, the slamming of a door, and loud, angry words too garbled to hear. It sounded serious.

Almost as one, the boys leapt to their feet and dashed out of the rec room towards the staircase. Carleton was already there, waving them back.

"Stay calm, everybody stay calm," he said. "For heaven's sake, don't come up unless I call you!"

Marl watched Carleton gallop up the stairs, his heart sinking.

When Carleton reached the second floor, the story lay in front of him. Fragments of a saucer and broken gingerbread cookies were strewn across the floor. Vilda leaned against the frame of the closed door, her kinky hair wild, her eyes glittering, near tears.

"I . . ." she tried to whisper, "I just . . ."

"Topo?" Carleton breathed. Vilda nodded shakily and the Englishman's jaw tensed. He knew what could happen when you tried to be nice to Topo. You were never sure if you'd get a shy smile or a plate flung at you. With Topo, nothing was certain.

"Sh, sh, dearie," Carleton soothed, "why don't you go downstairs and rest for a moment to settle your nerves?"

Vilda nodded again and made her way to the staircase, her hand on the wall to steady her.

The Englishman ran his hands through his thinning copper hair. The day had gone so well and now this!

But I should have expected as much, he thought. Whenever Topo felt left out of anything, even punishment, he became moody. The moods led to grumbling and sparks of anger that developed into an explosion over the smallest thing. A word, a sideways glance: It didn't take much to set him off.

This upset came at the worst possible time. Just after dinner, Carleton had received the follow-up call from Officer Rowan in the Drum. The Englishman had invited the policemen for a visit the next day, to show them how well the boys had met their punishment of cleaning the bus. It would be just like Topo to cause a scene to embarrass him in front of the officers. He had to settle this now. Carleton took a deep breath and rapped on the door.

"Laddie," he said carefully, "can I come in?"

"Don't you touch that goddamn door!"

Carleton bit his lip. Topo was still very angry and possibly still violent. Carleton had learned from experience that the boy needed to be handled gently when he was in such a mood.

"I think I should come in," the Englishman pressed gingerly. "I think we should have a chat."

In response, an object was hurled against the door, meeting its target with a crack! It sounded like a shoe. Carleton wondered if there was anything dangerous or breakable in the room. He tried to be a little firmer.

"Now you know, lad, it's not a good idea to stay by yourself . . . when you're depressed."

"I'm fine!" Topo shot back. "Just go away."

Carleton clenched his teeth and closed his eyes. It was hard to help someone who did not want to be helped. Today it seemed especially hard.

"Still, I have to try," the Englishman sighed to himself; "it's my duty." Perhaps there was more to Topo's behavior than he knew. He would attempt to find out.

Vilda heard Carleton start down the stairs and met him on the landing. Her eyes were red and her whole body drooped with weariness. Carleton felt bad about troubling her but there was no other way.

"Vilda, dear," he said gently, "was there anything said? I mean, do you have any inkling why . . . he's flown off the handle, this time?"

Vilda's mouth tightened and her chin pulled up a bit. How could she tell him what she'd said on the ridge of

Horsethief Canyon? She really was sorry that it had ever happened, and she had come to apologize to the boy. But he'd blown up at her and she didn't really blame him. She couldn't tell that to Carleton, though. It was a private thing between her and the boy.

"No," she said and cleared her throat. "No, I don't recall anything."

Carleton was nodding sympathetically. "All right, dear, I'll go back up and give it another try. Maybe he's just having a bad day."

As Carleton approached the closed door his pulse quickened nervously. For just a moment he stood in the hallway, afraid. He felt as if he'd been spread too thin, had taken on a bigger fight than he could ever hope to win. A selfish, human part of him said, Leave the boy alone, he'll cool down. But the sane, social worker part of him knew that he couldn't do that. Carleton had too much experience with disturbed children, boys and girls who couldn't contain their rage and turned it on themselves. He knew about the rippers; he'd seen the scars on the arms and legs of boys who'd passed through the farm. Carleton winced. Sometimes you never knew who was a ripper and who wasn't, until it was too late.

"Topo, it's me again," he said, in what he hoped was a reassuring way. "Lad, I'd like to come in."

No answer. A beat of panic pulsed through the Englishman's fingertips. He knocked again, faster.

"Are you there? I want to talk to you, Topo."

The silence seemed too large, too frightening. Terror seized Carleton; he grasped the knob and lunged in.

The boy flew at him from the right, catching the thin Englishman off guard in the semidarkness. Carleton gasped in surprise and hurtled to the floor, skidding across the polished hardwood until he slammed into the side of a bed. Pain speared his shoulder and in a moment Topo had dropped onto him. They grappled desperately.

"I warned you!" Topo hissed through clenched teeth.

This boy is strong! the Englishman gasped to himself.

Topo was roughly hewn and clumsy, but made of solid muscle, and he was not playing. Carleton felt panic rising in his throat as he struggled to get out from under the boy. He was holding back Topo's arms but one of them slipped, and smacked Carleton painfully across the jaw.

Enough! the man's mind roared in fury. With a surge of strength he wrenched himself out from under the heavy boy and fumbled frantically to lock Topo's arms behind his back. Carleton was slight but quick, and eventually he lay gasping in the dimness, holding the boy tight in a full Nelson. The Englishman's legs were entwined around Topo's, holding them from doing any damage.

Good God, Carleton breathed to himself, a shudder of relief going through his body. Topo was cursing at him now but the steam seemed mostly to be gone. He sounded more hurt than angry.

"Laddie, laddie," Carleton sighed, "what's ado now?"

"Lemme go," the broad-backed boy said sullenly, and he twisted, trying to pull away. Carleton's jaw hurt and his head ached but he hung on.

"What's ado, lad? You've got to tell me."

Topo suddenly went limp against him. "Okay, okay," he grumbled, "just let go." With a pang of regret Carleton did and the husky boy pulled himself up, quickly turning his face away. He dropped onto his bed and sat, back to the wall, his knees drawn up. Wearily, Carleton sat down on the opposite bed, the question alight in his eyes.

Topo struggled with himself. He thought that the problem was Marl and just imagining the boy's diamond-shaped face made his skin burn and the collar of his shirt prickle with heat. It was a bad feeling, even for Topo who was used to bad feelings. But he didn't think he could tell anyone about it. Topo worked so hard to appear tough and grown up. He knew he had a reputation for being mean. What would the other boys say if they knew that some stupid little kid like Marl could rattle him? Topo swallowed and said nothing.

Carleton mopped his sweaty forehead, feeling angrier every moment.

Not an inch! he thought. He won't give me an inch or a single minute to help him. And now of all blasted times, with the police coming tomorrow! That very human part of Carleton began thinking how much easier it would be to run the farm without Topo. He could have it all under control if it weren't for this boy.

Carleton stood up. "All right, Topo, have it your way," he said, "but that was your last chance. Trip up again, on anything, and back you go." The Englishman paused for emphasis. "And best behavior tomorrow, lad," he warned. "We're having guests from the police department. Another performance like this one and I swear, I'll string you up by your ruddy thumbs."

The silence followed Carleton down the stairs. No one was waiting there, but then he hadn't expected it. He'd been through this before, he'd seen the effect that these blowups had. After the first stabs of curiosity, the others withdrew, sometimes for days.

Chased by their own devils, Carleton thought, and he looked into the rec room, where the boys stared as silently as zombies while the ghostly light of the television flickered over their faces.

Marl sat in a big chair in the gray light, his knees drawn up carefully, his elbows held close to his sides. The card game had been abandoned. No one was laughing, no one was even talking. The good feeling he'd had earlier had gone completely.

I want it back! his heart seemed to cry in his chest.

Goat was on the floor, arms wrapped around his knees, an island of a creature. The T.V. channel was turned to one of the many detective shows being rerun that summer. Shy and fumbling, Marl tried to bring back the good feeling that had been there earlier in the evening.

"Who do you think's the killer?" he asked.

Goat was glassy eyed, still caught up in the sounds he'd

heard over his head. Goat didn't like Topo much but a part of him was touched. There was no living peacefully next to pain, no living quietly beside hurt. It grabbed you and sent you hurtling down into your own dark hole. And in that hole, Goat heard Marl's voice, intruding on his thoughts. It grated on him and he didn't answer.

A little pulse of panic clutched at Marl's heart.

"Do you think that's the killer?" he asked again, more forcefully.

"Sh!" Goat hissed over his shoulder.

The sound was like a knife to Marl. Its harshness carved through him and he felt his insides contract in a spasm of pain. Marl had no experience with friends. He had no understanding of the ups and downs that made things interesting. To Marl, down was down.

Oh God, it meant nothing! he thought. The afternoon, the work they'd done together, everything. He was alone, he would always be alone. Marl saw the rec room through a brimming blur and in his ears he heard a familiar voice.

"I hate to do this, Marl," Cecile had said, staring at him intently, "but there aren't any foster homes available. You have to go into Ryerson for a while."

Marl remembered it vividly. It had happened last year, when he was eleven, in an office at Family Services.

"Why don't you take me?" he'd asked suddenly. "If you really don't want me to go back, you could take me."

Cecile didn't say anything for a moment and Marl's heart leapt, thinking that she was considering it.

"I could be your kid," he said hopefully and Cecile seemed to wince.

"I can't, Marl."

"Why not?"

"It . . . just doesn't . . . work that way." Cecile was struggling with every word. "Family Services doesn't allow . . ."

"But you could ask," Marl pleaded. "Nobody would get mad if you just asked."

Cecile shook her head, her mouth drawn into a thin

line, as if she were in pain. There was no hope in her face and Marl turned so that he was staring at the wall. He was trembling. Cecile was all he had. If she didn't love him, then nobody did, and they never would.

That's when he had done it. Three days later in the basement bathroom at Ryerson, Marl had taken the sharp lid of a tin can and carved the long slashes into the calf of his left leg.

In the rec room of the Jenner farm, Marl felt numb. Nobody, not Goat, not even Cecile was going to save him from his train dream. It was a dangerous, deadly ride but once you were on it, there was no stopping. Until you were there. Then you would stop.

8

"Hey . . . Marl!" The voice came from a dark shape just outside the kitchen screen door and Marl paused, clutching his broom. He was on after lunch sweeping duty, but he'd waited until Brucie and Goat had finished the dishes and disappeared. He'd been alone, until now.

"What?" Marl said. The angle of the sun made it hard to tell who the shape was but it had a lumbering, brooding appearance. Marl guessed and he guessed right.

"C'mere," Topo said. Marl took a few cautious steps forward, trailing the broom behind him. Topo made him wary: Marl hadn't forgotten the potato garden. He noted that the screen door opened outwards. That was good. It would give him an extra half second if Topo lunged for him.

Topo didn't lunge. When Marl was close enough the chestnut-haired boy reached into his pocket and pulled out a small bottle with a black and white label. He held it close to his side so that it could be jammed back into his pocket with a quick thrust. Marl peered closer, recognizing the shape of the bottle instantly. Typewriter correction fluid. For a moment he simply stared but then Topo sniffed dramatically and smiled.

"Wanna come get a little buzz on?" he asked.

It was a conspirator's smile and it included Marl, wrapping around him like a friendly arm. Standing there, his hands sweating on the long broom handle, Marl could feel a tug-of-war pulling his insides apart.

Don't, said a voice in his head that sounded like Cecile. Marl, you promised to be good.

Marl remembered the promise with a pang, but Cecile didn't know what it was like! You couldn't count on anything, Marl thought savagely. You couldn't count on anyone or anything to stay the way it was supposed to. A bitter taste welled up in his mouth. He tried not to think about the night before, but the leftover feelings throbbed, raw and painful as a gash. Being good never got you anywhere, Marl wanted to tell Cecile. It never got you anything important. You still got stomped on. Being good never got you friends, or let you keep them.

Marl swallowed. "Yeah, okay," he told Topo. The other boy put the bottle back in his pocket and looked left and right.

"Get a bag from the drawer," he instructed Marl softly.

Marl leaned the broom against a wall and rummaged quietly until he found a paper bag, then stuck it under his shirt. He slipped out the screen door, letting it close gently on his fingers.

"Where'd you get it?" he asked, squinting in the bright noon light as he trotted alongside Topo.

"Sh!" Topo kept looking nervously over his shoulder. "Jenner's study. He's always typing stuff."

There were no more questions, just the gentle scuffing of their feet over the burnt prairie and the slight crackle of the paper bag under Marl's shirt. Under the shirt and the bag Marl's heart was thudding a tattoo against his chest. He hoped Topo couldn't tell.

The tall brawny boy led Marl around the side of the house. With a start, Marl realized Topo meant to go into the bus, which had been parked on the grass close to the water hose. His one good afternoon flew back at him like a cruel joke and he halted, not wanting to go in.

Topo slid open the shiny side door and glared at Marl. "Well, come on," he whispered fiercely. The sound pushed Marl past the point of no return and up the small step into the bus. It was like a furnace inside. All the windows were closed and the hot air scorched Marl's throat. Even the seats and the chrome were hot when he touched them. Topo dropped to his knees and crawled his way to the back of the bus where it was darker. The screens on the rear window were like venetian blinds and the sun fell in crazy strips on the floor and on the boys jammed between the seats.

Topo stuck out his hand and Marl passed him the paper bag, watching as the large boy deftly coated the inside with the fluid.

It's different, Marl thought sadly. There was no light talk between them, no good-natured kidding or easy silence. There was only the bag.

Topo rolled down the brown paper edges; the crackling seemed as loud as thunder. He looked up and a slash of light caught him across the forehead, giving his eyes an unearthly glitter.

"You first," Topo said, and he handed Marl the bag.

Officer Dan Rowan was counting farmhouses. "One, two, three," he muttered softly to himself. "First right after the Grier farm?" he asked his partner.

Jeffery Bleans scanned the directions he'd written on a tiny pad. "Yup," he said and Dan swung the police car off the smooth highway and onto a grid road. The gravel rumbled under their tires.

"Have you ever been to . . . one of these places?" Jeffery asked suddenly. He was strapped in by his safety belt but he still seemed to be perched on the edge of his seat.

"Oh, once or twice," Dan Rowan said, shrugging his huge shoulders. "There's another one of these group homes just outside the town of Hanna."

"Oh," Officer Bleans said. Dan had already explained the reason for this trip and Jeffery had been eager to go. He hadn't expected to be so nervous, though. He was glad they had no jurisdiction here, beyond the city limits of

Drum. They were still in uniform but it made their visit seem less official and more friendly. Jeffery Bleans wanted to appear friendly to the boys.

The Jenner farm seemed to come up out of nowhere, its rusty red roof a blaze on the prairie.

"Guess we're here," Officer Rowan said, and he pulled into the long driveway. They walked up to the house but didn't have the chance to knock on the front door.

"Hello, hello," Carleton greeted them, "splendid you could come. Lads, you all remember Officer Rowan and Officer Bleans?"

The young policeman smiled shyly and the boys in the living room stared back woodenly, defiant. They couldn't give that look to Dan Rowan, though. His towering shape and dark eyes were imposing and demanded respect. Goat especially felt the strength of the policeman's eyes and he shrank from it. Today the hollow tiredness was back, and he didn't know why.

"I say, a tour might be in order," Carleton said cheerily, and he led the constables around the house and garden, listing the chores that the boys did, pointing out the wooden things they had made.

"Cal built that," the Englishman said, pointing to a small table. "So good with his hands! He'll be a craftsman one day, perhaps."

The boys, who had been following curiously at a distance, rolled their eyes.

Finally, when he realized he couldn't keep the two officers any longer without being rude, the Englishman cleared his throat.

"Now it's time for the grand finale," Carleton announced. "I'm going to show you what incredible work these boys can do when they put their minds to it. Gentlemen, it's time to see the bus."

Marl's nose burned and his mouth was numb, as if someone had punched him. When he rubbed his eyes they smarted, so he tried not to do it, but he kept forgetting and hurting himself. He felt entirely alone in his haze although he knew Topo was very near. He didn't look at Topo much: The boy's hazel eyes seemed to reach out for him shining eerily. Other things would catch his attention, the chrome on the seats, a patch of light, and Marl would be captured, not able to look away. How long had they been crouched in the back of the bus? Marl didn't know. It couldn't have been more than an hour but it felt like a day.

Suddenly Topo stood up. "I gotta get something," he said, moving away. Marl's heart leapt into a gallop.

"What's wrong?" he asked, fear edging his voice.

"Nothing." Topo was stealthily sliding open the side door. "You just stay there. I'll be back."

But Marl wasn't sure. He cold feel a throbbing in his throat and his temples. Was somebody coming? Was that it? He strained to listen but he knew he wasn't hearing properly. Topo had sounded as though he were talking through cotton gauze. Should he stand up, run? Marl tried to get up but pain shot through his legs; he'd been sitting too long. The bus seemed as tight as a coffin. It felt as if the walls were folding in on him.

I gotta get out of here! Marl thought wildly but he couldn't move. His heart was racing with a frightening thud, thud, and he could feel the sweat beading on his forehead. Where was Topo? How long had he been gone?

"Oh God," Marl whispered. His eyes were wet and smarting.

Just then, he did hear something. It sounded like the burbling of a stream but Marl knew there were no streams on the prairie. It had to be people! Panicking, he clutched around him, but the bag was gone, maybe jammed under a seat. What if someone found it? The voices were getting louder!

Marl heard the latch and the grating of the door as it slid open. It seemed to take years and he was frozen to the floor. Bang, bang, bang! his heart pounded. He had to get out!

"They even steam cleaned the seats," Carleton said proudly, stepping inside. Volts of electricity seemed to burst through Marl, throwing him to his feet in a surge of pain.

"Marl?" Carleton asked, his eyes widening. Marl gasped and fell, the bus swirling before the blackness swallowed him.

"Great Scott!" Carleton cried and he dropped beside the fallen boy. Dan Rowan, who so easily took charge, took charge again. He bounded up into the bus and in a moment he was searching for a pulse and pulling open Marl's eyelids.

"Jeff—doctor!" He cried over his shoulder. Officer Bleans leapt into a run, pushing aside the boys who had clustered around the door. Topo fell back, as weightless as straw.

"Oh, my God!" he breathed, horrified. He'd come with the group from the house, anxious to see Marl get caught. This wasn't supposed to happen. He'd only meant to get Marl into trouble. He'd never meant to kill him!

"What is it?" Carleton shook the policeman's arm in worry.

"I don't know," Dan Rowan said grimly. "Drugs, I think." He looked at Marl's reddened nose and mouth, too raw for sunburn. "An inhalant, but I don't know what kind."

The Englishman began searching around the seats, and finding something, thrust it in front of Officer Rowan. The empty bottle of typewriter correction fluid lay in the bottom of the bag but Dan Rowan didn't have to see it. Just opening the bag he recognized the heady scent.

"Damn!" he muttered to himself, and his hands flew to Marl's neck, trying to measure the pulse again.

"What, what?" Carleton was frantic.

"He could be having heart palpitations," Dan Rowan said. "The fluid reacts with chemicals in the body to accelerate the heart. Kids have had heart attacks, because they tried to run after inhaling. Fright and flight. This stuff is the devil," he whispered bitterly.

Carleton was biting his lip, running his hand over Marl's

sweat-soaked back. "Laddie, laddie," he murmured. Hearing a noise he whirled around and looked over his shoulder.

"Get back, all of you!" he snapped. "Go to the house and stay there." The strain showed in his voice and the sharpness of his tone drove them back. The boys began drifting reluctantly towards the house.

"I've heard of falling down on the job . . ." Len started.

"Just shut the hell up, Len!" Topo snarled, cutting him off. "Just shut your goddamn mouth."

Len glanced at Topo's bulky frame and clenched fists. The threat was very real. He swallowed whatever else he had to say.

The tiredness had fallen away from Goat and all his muscles were tensed, ready to spring. Once inside, he fled up the stairs two at a time and rushed into his empty room to stand by the window. Like a sentry Goat stood guard, his stormy-sea eyes fixed on the Volkswagen's roof, his fingernails digging into the window frame.

By the time the doctor arrived, Marl had come to and so he was put into his bed instead of an ambulance.

"But that's not to say this wasn't close," the doctor warned Carleton sternly. "It's just to say we've been lucky, this time. If he'd had the chance to break into a run, I could be calling you from the morgue. You can't leave solvents or inhalants just lying around, especially here."

Carleton stood, his hands clasped.

"I . . . I use it for my typing," he rambled. "You need these things about and . . . and it's so difficult to watch them all, all of the time . . ."

The doctor only shook his head, closed up his bag, and left.

Dan Rowan and Jeffery Bleans had been standing back, out of the way, but now Dan Rowan stepped forward.

"Mr. Jenner," he said, his hands curling around his belt, "how many adult supervisors do you have on the farm?"

It was a question Carleton had expected, and dreaded.

"Well, there's myself and Vilda. We're here all the time."

Vilda shot Carleton a sharp look. She considered herself a cook, not a supervisor. Officer Rowan was nodding thoughtfully.

"Have you ever considered getting more help?" he asked.

"What?" the Englishman exclaimed. "No, never! I mean, I don't think that's really necessary. Most days are very, very good. This and the bus are highly unusual incidents, you understand?"

Dan Rowan's steady look said that he did understand, far too well. When the officers were leaving, Jeffery Bleans stopped and leaned his back against the door frame.

"Mr. Jenner," he started, his young face intense and earnest, "please remember, if you need anything . . . we're . . . Officer Rowan and I . . ."

"I'll remember," Carleton said, ushering them out. "Thank you, thank you for everything! Drive carefully!"

When he pulled back into the yellow light of the kitchen, his face was haggard. Vilda looked up and saw the weariness. She sucked in her breath. In that moment she thought she understood the Englishman and his desperation. It was a pity to see a grown man plead the way Carleton had been obliged to with the policemen. But what could she possibly do? She was only a cook. It wasn't her place or her privilege to say anything. Vilda wiped her hands on her apron and turned away.

Marl lay on his back in bed, staring at the beams of the ceiling. It was getting late; the light in his room was tinged with pink. Beside him on a table there was a pitcher of ice water and he listened to the ice cubes tinkle as they melted and settled.

Oh, God, he thought, clenching the sheet under him, everything was such a mess! It wasn't supposed to turn out like this. Not today, not any day. He'd come to the farm really meaning to try but it was all so jumbled up now.

July was at its deadly worst on the second floor of the

Jenner farm, but Marl felt a cold chill clamp around him; his fingertips were icy against his thighs.

It's me, he knew. Nothing he did ever worked out, not even when he tried to be good. Something was very wrong with him, and it was more than his strange, slanted eyes. Why else would everybody abandon him? Cecile, Goat, and even Topo could see what was the matter with him. They just weren't telling him. Was it the way he looked, or what he said? Why couldn't anybody ever like him? Why couldn't . . .

Marl started, a twitch that rustled the sheets. He felt the presence rather than seeing it. When he did look up, Goat was there, leaning against the door frame.

Goat's thumbs were hooked through his belt loops and he was staring up at the crack where the boards in the door frame met.

"That was pretty goddamn stupid, you know," he said.

Marl's nose had begun to trickle and he sniffled. "Yeah, well, that's the way it goes," he said, trying to keep his voice light even though his breath was coming in short gasps. "You take your chances."

For a long moment Goat said nothing and Marl felt a little jab of anger.

"It's hard to lay your hands on really good stuff around here," he said casually. "You know, like this . . ."

"Oh, cut the crap, Marl," Goat spat the words, turning so that his eyes held Marl in a steely grip. "Do you know what that stuff can do to your guts? Or your heart, or your nervous system? I know two guys who are six feet under and another one who's tied to a bloody wheelchair because they blew their brains on cheap highs. You might as well drink Lysol, for Christ's sake!"

Marl swallowed. He hadn't expected this. He hadn't expected it at all.

"So you're no angel in white," he said, the words rushing out in a whisper.

"But I'm not stupid!"

"Neither am I!" Marl shot back. "Get off my case."

Goat had been moving closer and in a spasm he turned to the window, his jaw set. Dusk was setting in now, and the shadows in the room were lengthening by the moment. They drew long lines on the tall boy's already lined face, deepening his creases and darkening the scar.

"You're not a kid here," Goat said finally. "Nobody's gonna take your hand and say 'don't do this,' 'don't do that.' Okay, so you don't care. That's fine, except . . ." Goat's eyebrows gathered as he continued, "except you ruin yourself. And they don't have to look at you forever. But you do."

The words hit Marl softly and spread, like rain on canvas. Under the sheet, the white lines on his leg throbbed.

"Do you think they'll ship me back to Ryerson?" he asked.

Goat blinked, considering. "No," he said, letting out a big breath, "Jenner comes on tough, but he's got this real big soft spot, especially for new kids. And I don't think he wants anybody to know . . . when things go wrong."

The wiry boy looked back at Marl. "Where'd you get it, anyhow?"

"I didn't," Marl said. "It just sorta showed up." He couldn't tell Goat about Topo. Sure, Topo had abandoned him, but it was a sacred rule. You never told on anybody else.

Goat knew that. A grin crinkled the left half of his face. "Oh sure, aliens landed and said, 'Hey, Marl, let's go get buzzed.' "

Marl smiled, settling himself comfortably on his elbows. "Yeah, that's how it happened."

"Great. Tell it to the judge."

They talked until the room was dark. It's so easy! Marl thought in awe. It had come back so easily: They threw words back and forth like a leisurely game of catch. All the bad events of the day drifted away, receding like a tide. Finally Goat stood up.

"I gotta go," he said, sauntering towards the door.

"Yeah, see ya."

The pillow whizzed out of nowhere, a blur of white that caught Marl on the side of the head with a whump!

"I owed you," Goat grinned from the door. Then he leapt aside as another pillow blasted the wall where he'd stood. Marl lay back, a laugh sitting in his throat like a bubble.

9

"You got off easy!" Goat exclaimed, his gray-blue eyes widening. "Last time I caught it, he had me waxing the flippin' floors."

Marl would gladly have waxed floors, or hoed a garden, or cleaned a bus. He would rather have sweat working out in the sun or given up T.V. privileges – anything other than the punishment Carleton had chosen.

"It's a simple thing, laddie," the Englishman had said quietly, leaning forward at his desk in the study. "All the resource materials are right here, or as close as the phone. I don't need anything fancy, just a simple report, like one you'd do for school. 'The Abuse of Common Household Products' could be the title. Mind you, I don't want a list." Carleton swept his hand towards the bookcase that held the encyclopedias. "I want you to give evidence of the damage these products can do."

Marl's eyes were glazed with horror. This project was a nightmare, the row of encyclopedias as forbidding as a mountain. He could only stare back at the Englishman with his mouth clamped shut, his stomach swaying sickly. Carleton misunderstood.

"Now, I know it's summer and the other lads won't have schoolwork until the tutor arrives in the fall, but I personally think this is very fair." Carleton looked irritated.

"Of course, you have a choice. There is always a choice.

You can do this report for me or we can call Cecile and the director of Family Services and let them decide."

He's bluffing, Marl though rapidly, he has to be. Goat had told him Careton hated to call outside help. But what if he wasn't? Marl tried to swallow the hard knot in his throat. He couldn't take the chance.

"Okay." The word sounded like a creak. "Okay, I'll do it."

The Englishman breathed a small sigh of relief to himself. "Good, good lad! I think you'll learn from it." He shuffled the papers on his crowded desk and scribbled down a number on a small piece of yellow paper.

"Here," he said, handing it to Marl, "this is the number of those nice officers who . . . who helped us yesterday. I'm sure they'd be glad to tell you which products are the most notorious. Then all you need to do is look them up."

Marl said nothing and left, the yellow paper burning his palm. Carleton watched him go, puzzled.

"You can whip this thing up tonight," Goat was saying, running his hand through his spiky blonde hair. "Christ, you could whip it up this afternoon!"

Marl was staring numbly at his knuckles. The yellow paper was folded into a tiny square and he clenched it tightly in his left hand. How could he tell Goat? How could he tell anyone? They thought a report was nothing. Goat was even laughing about it. If he told, Goat would be laughing at him too.

"It's a simple thing," Carleton had said.

Right, Marl thought, real simple. Except if you can't read.

Carleton had been puzzled about Marl's reaction to the punishment but he didn't puzzle long. He was panicking. Right now, the boy was only a small worry; Carleton's mind was on the police. He could just imagine the things they were saying after they left the farm.

"Two supervisors to ten boys?"

"Can't control them."

"Doesn't know what's going on."

"Shouldn't someone be aware of this?"

The Englishman was trembling. He knew they were right; that was the horror of it. Vilda didn't count; ten boys to one adult was too much. He'd known it for a long time. He also knew that if he didn't take steps, someone would take them for him. The might shut down the farm for good.

"Eight," Carleton thought frantically, "I could manage with eight." After ten, eight would be a snap. He scanned the papers that lay in front of him. As luck would have it, Cal was being placed in a foster home at the end of the month. That left just one: One boy would have to go.

Carleton toyed with his pencil until it snapped and then started twisting paper clips. No matter whom he chose, it wouldn't be fair. There were reasons for keeping, or sending back, any one of them. Goat, because he was the oldest, or Marl, because he was new. Len, because he was mouthy, or Pete, because he was young and could probably get placed somewhere. No, there wasn't a clear choice; but the choice was clear in Carleton's mind. Sometimes you had to sacrifice the one for the many. He knew which one he was going to sacrifice.

Topo leaned against the side of the house that was shaded, sweat dampening in a V on the front of his T-shirt. He held a number of stones in his large, calloused hands: He'd scooped them up from the driveway, planning on hurling them one by one at the rickety old toolshed. It was one of the few things he liked to do. He liked the way the stones zinged across the yard and it gave him a sense of satisfaction to see the cracks he'd put in the rotting boards. It helped if you threw things, Topo thought.

But not today. He was in his regular spot with a good supply of sharp-sided rocks, but all he could do was tumble them gently from one hand to another. He didn't have the energy, or the anger, for target practice.

"It's that kid," Topo murmured. Marl was draining him. He tried to put the previous day out of his mind but he kept seeing Marl's small, neat body laid out on the floor of the bus. It was a hard memory, even for Topo, who was used to hard memories.

"Not my fault," Topo muttered to himself, but those old familiar words didn't work this time. Sure, Marl was okay, but what if he hadn't been? What if he'd wound up a vegetable or something? Sweat trickled off Topo's forehead and into his eyes. He blinked painfully.

What if Marl had wound up . . . dead? Topo felt his insides quiver. There had been talk like that, after the doctor arrived and before anyone knew what was going on. When he'd heard that Marl was okay, he'd felt an exhilarating rush of relief. Relief was a strange sensation to Topo, but he liked it. He even liked remembering it. For the first time in a long time, he wished he had somebody to talk to. Topo let the stones slide through his fingers and drop onto the dirt.

Marl wasn't such a bad kid, he reflected, ambling into the farmhouse. Maybe they could talk sometime. Maybe, somehow, they could be friends.

Marl didn't like Topo at all just then. By supper, he hated him. Carleton had cleared a space on his desk and locked his cabinets, allowing Marl to work in the study. Marl sat, staring bitterly at the papers in front of him hating Topo.

"He got away clean," Marl thought darkly. "It was his idea and he got away clean and now I'm the one stuck doing this garbage."

It was a slow torture, although he'd done what he could. He'd forced himself to unfold the little yellow paper and phone the police station, luckily getting Officer Bleans on the first try. Marl was shy at first but Jeffery Bleans was so friendly and helpful that Marl wasn't afraid to ask him to spell the names, letter by letter. He'd copied them down and now his own cramped printing stared back, taunting him.

Actually, Marl could read, but not much. He could read

the baby words he'd memorized in grade one and two: The "cat" and "pat" kind of words were very clear to him. Beyond that, everything was blurred. It was in grade three that the letters wouldn't hold still anymore in his head and the silent vowels became a complete mystery. Cecile had gotten him into special classes for kids who had trouble reading and writing but somehow it had been really easy to goof off without getting caught. It hadn't seemed to matter.

It mattered now. Marl tried sounding out the words, letter by letter, but he kept getting lost, becoming angrier by the minute.

"Goddamn Topo," he muttered, because hating Topo was easier than doing anything else right now. When the supper gong sounded, Marl jumped up and fled, running as if from a bad dream.

Everyone at the table seemed happy and that irked Marl. Their chatter bounced around the room and Marl sank down, leaning on his elbow.

"Manners!" Carleton exclaimed irritably, giving Marl a solid shake by the shoulder. The boy pulled himself up, faintly glad that someone else wasn't having such a great day either.

There was a reason for Carleton's bad mood and his pointed English jaw was set in a determined way, as if he were taking a spoonful of medicine. He left right after supper and no one knew where he was going.

"I'll be back by eleven or so," he told Vilda. "You can handle the fort for a few hours, can't you, dearie?" Vilda felt herself filling with dread at being alone with the boys, but Carleton looked so serious. He was clutching an armful of files in front of him like a shield, carefully hiding the name that was on them.

"I guess I can manage," she said rather weakly, then held up a finger at the boys who were still at the table.

"Not one peep," she warned them, "not one peep of trouble do I want to hear outta you. No bickering, no roughhousing. And you keep that T.V. turned down!"

"They'll be good lads," Carleton said softly before he left. "They really are good lads."

"Don't bother with the dishes," Vilda cried, shooing the boys out of the kitchen. "I'll do 'em tonight. Just go on and stay outta my hair."

No one was going to argue with that, especially Rayo and Cal who were on clean up duty that night. Chairs scraped, silverware clattered, and in a moment of scrambling footsteps, the kitchen was deserted. Vilda sniffed, pushed away a sweaty tuft of hair, and set to the work she knew so well.

From a hook in the broom closet she pulled out a blue and white striped apron and tied it around her wide hips. She turned on the taps to fill the sink and began scraping dishes stacking them. Uneaten morsels of food glared at her from the plates.

"Hmph!" she grumbled to herself. "Half the world's starving and they're leavin' good food on their plates to be thrown away. Kids today don't know what it is to go hungry!"

The sink was almost overflowing and she hurried over to turn off the water.

"Glasses first," she said, as if she were giving lessons. They clinked, settling into the suds in a comfortable, familiar way. Vilda didn't mind doing dishes. In fact, she didn't mind any of the chores on the Jenner farm.

"If only it weren't for *them*," she thought, "I wouldn't have a complaint in the world." Right now *they* were safely out of her way, ruining their eyes in front of the T.V., and Vilda felt almost contented. The evening sun painted her chubby face with a yellow glaze, the deep yellow that always comes before sunset. She was just reaching for the first pots when the phone rang.

"Oh, bother," Vilda said aloud, wiping her hands on her apron. Topo halted in his tracks, standing soundlessly in the darkened hallway. He'd been on his way to get a glass of orange juice but now he stopped, listening. Phone calls were rarely for the boys on the farm, but they were often about them. It was always a good idea to pick up what you could.

Vilda took the receiver off the wall phone and clamped it under her chin. "Hello?"

There was a beat of silence and then Topo heard a slight gasp.

"A-Adele?" Vilda's voice quavered. It obviously wasn't about him, but Topo couldn't go. Her shocked voice made him curious and he leaned against the wall, just out of the light.

"My Lord, it's been a long time, honey," Vilda said, running her hand nervously through her hair. "How . . . how did you get this number?"

Peeking out past the curve of the doorway, Topo could see Vilda nodding.

"Oh, this is where I work," Vilda said. "It's sorta this group home for foster kids." Her eyebrows furrowed. "No, they're not like that. They're nice."

A wave of surprise pulsed through Topo and he leaned closer, dangerously close to the edge of the door.

"It's good to hear from you, honey," Vilda said softly. "How've you been?" As she listened, the creases seemed to deepen around her eyes and mouth. "A job in the city? What kind of job? Who will you stay with?"

Topo saw Vilda flinch; the caller clearly did not like the questions. The cook kept trying to cut in again.

"A guy . . . what kind of . . . how long? . . ." Vilda's hands clenched the receiver.

"I'm not gettin' tense, Adele; just listen to me! You gotta be careful. I read about things in the paper all the time. There are so many crazies running around these days. You're young, you don't know . . ." She paused, cut off again. When she spoke her voice was a pained whisper.

"Adele, you're all I got. Of course I worry. I hate seein' you run around like some kind of . . . No, no! Don't go, not yet. I didn't mean it. Look, why don't you come out for a visit? We could get this all straight. Adele, honey? . . ." Vilda pleaded, then she shut her eyes tightly.

The receiver dropped to chest, where she clasped it for a moment. When she finally turned to replace it, blinking tears, she saw him.

Topo had inched out half into the doorway and he stood there, frozen. If he understood anything, he understood hurt, and this was a hurt so raw it touched even him. He couldn't look away.

Vilda was horrified that someone should find her like this. She drew herself up as tall as she could, sniffling, swallowing.

"What do you want?" she asked brusquely.

Topo simply stood there, looking old in his young body. "Is she . . . your kid?"

Vilda listened for sarcasm in his voice but there was none. She hadn't expected this gentleness and it caught her off guard. "She's mine," she said nervously, clutching at her apron.

"I'm sorry," Topo said softly. "I'm real sorry. For the other day, for everything."

And he was, the cook could see it in his clear eyes. A sob escaped her and she choked back another in her throat. There he was, she thought, this *hoodlum*, saying what she should have said, days ago.

"I didn't mean it, Lord, no I didn't," the words tumbled out of Vilda breathlessly. "At the canyon . . . you understand. I got so much on my mind, I can hardly sleep some nights. I'm talkin' without thinking and Lord, I don't mean it at all."

She sighed and wiped under her eye with a knuckle. "The things I say, they always did get me in trouble."

"Yeah," the boy said, "me too."

The day was fading fast now and the kitchen seemed rosy from the setting sun.

"So," Vilda smiled weakly, "what do you want, really?"

"Orange juice," Topo said. "I'll get it." His stockinged feet were as soundless as a ghost on the tile. When he'd closed the fridge door her hand reached out, jerkily, and rested on his shoulder.

82

It was warm, Topo realized with a jolt; it was a warm hand. It seemed to push back the loneliness just a bit and he stood still for a moment longer, feeling the warmth flow into him like a small current. It stayed with him even after he'd left and joined the others in the rec room. Two good feelings in the same day! Maybe it was a sign of calmer times, of better times. He felt hopeful.

10

There was no hope in the study. Right after supper Marl steeled himself and marched through the door to face the dreaded books. Bravely he hauled out one of the encyclopedias and tried looking up the first word on his list, slowly tracing under each letter with his finger. There was a small moment of triumph when he found it, but it dissolved into utter despair when he saw the thick, close-set paragraphs that filled the page. Even if by some miracle he could copy the whole page, Carleton would know he hadn't written it himself.

Marl stared at the encyclopedia page until his eyes blurred and there was a dull, throbbing pain behind his eyes. Struggling with books was so familiar to him. He felt he'd been doing it all his life.

"Marl, stop wasting time. This work is easy!"

"What's the matter, Marl? You're holding up the rest of the class."

"Stop being lazy! You could read this if you'd only try."

But I did try! he wanted to cry. I did!

He remembered how the other kids had laughed and called him stupid. Nothing was worse than reading aloud. His fumbling and guessing made the teachers angry and everyone else snickered and whispered. That's when he started acting up to get out of class, and he stopped telling people he didn't understand.

So what if they think I'm stupid, Marl thought. They already do anyway.

It was a dark side of him, not being able to read, and Marl kept it secret. He knew how. In the close, beehive life at Ryerson there were a lot of things you never admitted to, like being a ripper. The way you hurt or helped yourself was your own business. Not telling kept you safe.

But he wasn't safe here. If he didn't do something Goat and everyone would think he was dumb. Cecile would find out about yesterday! Marl crumpled sheets of paper and threw them at the wall. He wanted to scream! It was all there, right in front of him. He just couldn't get at it!

That's when Goat opened the study door and poked his head in. "Hey, aren't you done? 'Vice Squad' is on."

"No, I'm not done!" Marl threw the words out bitterly and Goat drew himself up, suddenly on guard.

"What's eating you?" he asked.

"Nothing. Go away, already."

But Goat would not go away. He slipped inside the room and leaned against the door. "Come on, what's wrong?" he asked again.

Marl's face was burning and his hands were clenched into fists on his knees. He'd been fighting this battle so long he didn't know how to stop. He gritted his teeth and said nothing.

Goat didn't understand. "Hey, don't take it so hard," he said helpfully. "It's no big deal."

Marl whirled around in the swivel chair, his eyes burning fiercely.

"Just shut up! Can't you ever shut up? Christ, how do you know what it's like? You go around shooting off your goddamn mouth and you don't know anything!"

"Hey, wait a minute," Goat tried to cut in, but Marl was attacking, in the same way he'd been attacked so many times.

"It's no big deal, right? It's easy! Everything's so bloody easy to you that you can go around giving everybody advice like . . ."

"I'll give you some advice right *now*!" Goat pointed, threatening.

"Yeah, you do that," Marl spat. "You're so smart you tell me how I'm supposed to write this goddamn thing if I can't read!"

Marl stopped, choking back the fury. He'd said it, he'd told! He hadn't meant to but the words rushed out, unstoppable. He felt a blow like a knee in his gut and he slumped to the desk, his hands over his eyes.

Goat stared. His hand was still raised and he lowered it, slowly. This was a new Marl, someone tougher and angrier than he'd expected. The words were soaking into him slowly.

"What?" Goat breathed. "Who said you can't read?"

"I just can't," Marl mumbled through his hands. He sounded exhausted.

"Why not?"

"How the hell should I know? I just can't." Marl took a deep breath. "Everything doesn't hold still in my head. Some things look like other things and it gets all screwed up."

Goat bit his lip thoughtfully. "So tell Jenner."

Marl's hands dropped and an almond eye pierced through Goat like a skewer. "Would you if it was you?"

"No," Goat answered honestly. "No."

Marl sighed but with his tiredness there was relief. The dull throbbing behind his eyes was gone. He felt a little better.

"So what are you going to do?" Goat asked.

"I don't know," Marl said.

"Can you read anything? I mean, a bit?"

"Yeah . . . no. Not enough," Marl said, flicking the sheets in front of him. He explained the list, and how he had written it down over the phone.

"You can understand if somebody just talks to you?"

"Oh, Christ! Of course I can." The color of Marl's face deepened. "I'm not an idiot."

Goat didn't think he was. He was planning something.

"I'll read it to you," he said simply.

"No." Marl's heart skipped a beat. It was one thing to tell Goat he couldn't read; it was something else to show him. The struggling, the fumbling—he couldn't let anyone see that. Marl felt the collar of his shirt choking him.

"Sure," Goat continued. "I'll read it and you pick out what fits and put it down. I'll spell what you don't know."

"No, I can't." The words were quick as a reflex.

Goat's patience was at an end. He threw up his hands and made to go.

"You think this is easy?" Marl blurted out. "You think this is easy to say?" His skin prickled and his stomach heaved as if he was going to be sick. Marl would have given anything right then to let Goat go. But there was no other way, and he knew it. Marl grabbed a thick encyclopedia and dropped it at the edge of the desk.

"There," he whispered, turning away. "Go ahead. Start."

That's how they managed it. Carleton was later coming home than he'd promised, and it was just as well. The boys worked until the deep night, their legs cramping, their bodies filming with sweat. Sentence by sentence Marl got it down, word by word he won the struggle.

"Pal . . . pal . . ."

"Palpitations." Goat was quiet, careful.

"Palpitations of the heart . . ." Marl would say faintly, and look up. "That's like tremors, right?"

"Right."

"T . . . r . . ." Marl would murmur to himself, concentrating so hard that Goat could stare at him openly.

"It's here," Goat thought. It was in Marl too. The stench of shame was here in this room and Goat knew it, the way an animal knows its own. And as he read the paragraphs, Goat sometimes faltered or gulped for air because his own pulse was pounding in his eardrums.

"Destroys?" Marl would ask shyly, glancing up then looking away.

"D-e-s . . ." Goat would reply softly, "t-r-o . . ."

The report was finished just after one o'clock. The boys

crept quietly out of the study and held their breath going up the stairs. Vilda seemed to have forgotten them; there was no sense reminding her. It was dark on the landing and Marl was glad.

"Thanks," was all he said before turning into his room. He laid the report on the night table and stared at it as he took off his clothes. The moonlight gave the pages a ghostly glow, but Marl knew they were real. Standing there in his shorts he touched the pages, feeling the indentations his words had pressed onto the paper. His words! He couldn't read them now, but they were *his*.

Marl brushed a hand across his eyes as he crawled into bed. He didn't know why, but they were burning.

Down the hall, Goat lay silently in his bed, listening to the others breathe, feeling the heat, feeling the weight. His pajama shirt was buttoned all the way to the top and he felt sticky and sweaty all over. He wanted to rip it open, tear the damn thing off! He wanted to fling back the blankets and run through the silver fields, covered only by the moonlight. But he couldn't. He couldn't undo so much as the first button. Goat remembered too clearly what people said when he wasn't covered.

He was small, in a place that was all white and sickly green and smelled so much that Goat wrinkled his nose. And there was a man with cold hands who sat Goat on a high, hard bed and said, "Good Lord, Willerton, come look at this."

Willerton came and with serious eyes they turned Goat over onto his thin stomach. They ran their hands over his legs, over his back, over the scars. Some were still sensitive and Goat winced, but he would not cry. He was ashamed because it was true, everything people told him was true. He was bad and now these men could see it too.

"Who brought him in?" Willerton asked.

"His teacher; he just started grade one."

Willerton's voice was soft, as if his throat hurt. "My God," he whispered, "grade one."

They sent a nurse in to stay with him and she held his

thin body tightly on her lap. The nurse began to cry because she was only human and she had children of her own. Goat watched her, dry eyed.

It was long ago but the images were still icy clear. Lying in his bed, Goat felt he understood Marl. He understood the anger that wouldn't go away. He knew the holes that eyes could burn in you, the people who talked about you as if you weren't there, as if you were dirt. And the boy who couldn't cry almost did. He had been alone for so long.

11

Cecile's mind was filled with Marl. When she left the city she was impatient with the early weekend traffic— she honked at a small gray Datsun for almost no reason at all. On the highway, she stabbed at the buttons of her car radio, switching from jazz to country to old-time fiddling before finally turning it off and listening to the hum of the air conditioner.

Marl! She didn't know what she'd find at the Jenner farm. The boy had seemed so hopeful and determined the day she left, and now this. Stealing a bus! When Carleton had telephoned to say that Marl had been involved in this escapade, she'd begun to worry. Even afterwards, when Carleton told her how well Marl had met his punishment, her worry persisted. Was Marl happy on the farm? Were things working out? They were questions she couldn't really ask; she had to see Marl's face to know the answers. Cecile knew this drive out to the farm was important. Her holidays began the next day, Saturday, and she couldn't fly off to the coast not knowing how Marl was.

Why was she finding it so hard to let go of this boy? Cecile had her other regular cases to keep her busy but she still found time to worry about Marl. She hadn't planned on missing him this much.

When she finally turned her car into the Jenner driveway, she blinked to clear her eyes. She didn't want anyone, especially Carleton, to know what she'd been thinking.

"Anyone home?" Cecile called politely, tapping at the kitchen door. Vilda was there in a moment, wiping the gleam from her forehead and inviting Cecile in.

"I'm in the hair-cutting business today." Cecile smiled and held up a small duffel bag.

"Well, Lord knows, it's time," Vilda said. "They're all startin' to look like shaggy dogs."

The two women moved the table out of the way and Cecile felt the warmth of familiarity. It was a homey kitchen, lived in but clean. She found herself thinking of her own mother's kitchen, how it smelled just as the bran muffins were coming out of the oven. It put her at ease.

In a moment, Carleton was in the doorway. "Splendid, splendid," he said softly, wringing his hands. "Delighted you could do this for us, Cecile."

Her good feeling about the kitchen spread to Carleton. He seemed to generate a caring quality: Cecile called it "good vibes." If something was troubling Marl, she didn't think it was Carleton.

Cecile unzipped her duffel bag and pulled out the scissors. "Bring them in whenever you're ready, Carl, one at a time."

Cecile knew most of the boys slightly and tried to put them at ease. Len was first and very much like himself.

"Hey, like I know you're busy." His tone was cool, worldly. "Why don't you just skip me today?"

Cecile pushed him gently into the chair. "What, and let you hide that good-looking profile? No way."

Len blushed to the roots of his sun-bleached hair and Cecile smiled a little as she began to cut. They boy's cockiness could survive anything except a compliment.

Topo was next, then Cal. A small, slight boy named Brucie had hollow eyes that worried Cecile: He seemed to be the pale gray color of something that was never out in the sun.

91

"So how are you today, kid?" she asked lightly, fingering his hair. It was as lifeless as dishwater.

"Oh, okay," the voice said, an incredibly small, empty voice. Cecile's heart leapt with a sense of danger. She realized that she wanted to see Marl *now*. She wanted to know that he was eating well, that he was getting enough sun. A panicky part of her wanted to know that Marl was not like Brucie. But she swallowed and began to cut carefully, filling the air with a bright chatter she didn't feel. She made a mental note to find out what she could about this boy, as soon as she could.

Marl was next and Cecile's worry melted away in a soft sigh. He was beautifully brown with a tan. His eyes seemed tired but they held a twinkle Cecile had never seen before. His dark hair was glossy and even his arms looked stronger. Cecile was so glad she could have hugged him, but she didn't. Two weeks away from her had made him a little shy, she could tell. She decided not to say anything about the bus, at least not right away.

She sat him down and walked around the chair, pretending to study him and feeling giddy.

"I went to a hairdressing school, you know," she said lightly. "Madam Zorba's Parlor of Elegance."

"Yeah, and you were so bad they kicked you out and you had to become a social worker," Marl said.

Cecile smiled wickedly. "Keep it up, Marl, and I'll give you a crew cut . . ."

"Or a mohawk!" a soft voice called out cheerfully.

Cecile looked up. The gaunt, straggly figure looked friendly but she didn't know who it was. Marl knew.

"Don't listen to that guy," he said. "He's been locked up so long he's gone crazy."

Marl heard the quiet padding of feet on the kitchen tile.

"He said he wanted to be a cop," Goat said, "so let's make him look like one."

Delight was dancing in Cecile's warm brown eyes.

"You just cut it up to here," Goat said, tracing a line that was high on the back of Marl's neck, "and you shave off everything underneath. They you cut a circle," he drew around Marl's ear, "and shave off everything in there."

The light touch tickled and Marl giggled. He pulled his head away, blushing, but Cecile was in on the game now.

"Okay," she smiled, "and we'll just take the rest of this"— she pulled up a long, thick lock of hair—"and crop it to there!" With her fingers she pretended to clip it next to his skull.

"No . . ."Marl was giggling, trying to pull away. He was embarrassed and surprised at being the center of attention.

The next moment Carleton was at the kitchen door, calling for Goat to help him move something, and Cecile and the boy were suddenly alone. She wanted to hug Marl, squeeze him and tell him she was so glad! Instead she ran her fingers through his shiny hair, thick as a pony's mane. Then she began to cut.

"So what have you been doing?" The shears ground and Cecile brushed a dark tuft onto the floor.

Marl started. How much did Cecile know? He decided to play it cool. "Oh, not much. We do chores and stuff."

"Like cleaning the bus?" she asked.

There was a pause and the boy's feet began swinging underneath the chair. "Yeah, that too."

"I hear you had a little ride," Cecile said.

"I wasn't the only one," Marl answered quickly and Cecile gently touched his ear.

"Keep still," she murmured. The swinging feet slowed.

"Where were you going to go?" she asked finally.

Marl shrugged. "I don't know. It was just . . . something to do."

Cecile could have gone into a lecture then, but somehow it wasn't in her. She was so glad to see him looking healthy and well and . . . what else? There was something about him, a sparkle. She wondered what it was. Marl seemed different, a little older, a little more confident. It came to her so suddenly she almost snipped her finger.

"Looks like you got a good friend there," she said casually.

"What?" The almond eyes widened.

Cecile tossed her head towards the kitchen back door. "That guy who was here."

"Goat," Marl said softly, a touch of wonder in his voice. They'd done a lot together, the bus, the report. But Marl had never put a name to it. He just knew that it was easy to talk to Goat. Maybe he'd told Goat more than he'd ever told anyone. And maybe, too, Goat didn't mind him being around. He'd helped last night, and before. Could Cecile see that? Did it show? Was it what Cecile said it was?

"Hey, I'm over here," Cecile was saying. "Hey, Marl."

She'd been talking to him and he hadn't even heard.

"What?"

She had stopped cutting and was leaning her hip against the kitchen table. "Do you think you'll be okay while I'm on holidays?"

"Oh sure," Marl said, tossing the words coolly off his shoulder.

"I'll be gone two weeks." Cecile let the words sink in. "I wouldn't want to go . . . if things weren't all right here."

Marl straightened his shoulders, feeling bigger somehow, feeling a hopeful tug inside him.

"Sure, you go on," he said, as if she had asked his permission. "I can take care of things, no sweat."

He felt taller sitting in that chair and he imagined that his shoulders were wider. He was trying to keep a straight face but instead he began to grin. And Cecile began to smile. And they stared, grinning at each other like the only two mice who know where the cheese is hidden.

When it was the next kid's turn, Marl stole shyly to the upstairs bathroom and closed the door. With his hands on the sink he peered into the mirror, blinking in awe at the stranger who stared back at him. Cecile had done an expert job, layering Marl's thick hair so that it flew away from his face. He couldn't believe it! He was the boy on the Cheerios box, a kid from T.V. You could barely notice his odd slanted eyes, or if you noticed them you wouldn't care.

Marl touched his face gingerly, as if it were fragile. He could be anybody. He could be somebody with a family and a dog and a real house. He could be a kid with friends.

His feet had a mind of their own and they ran him out of the bathroom, up and down the halls, over the beds.

"Don't run in the house!" The cry rumbled through the walls but Marl's feet didn't hear. They kept moving him, light, breathless, pattering like rain on a hot, dusty roof.

"What?" The voice was hoarse with disbelief. "What the hell are you saying?"

"Now, now lad, don't get yourself worked up." Carleton held up his hands nervously. "You might have guessed that this was coming."

Topo had not guessed; his narrowed eyes were horrified.

Carleton tried again. "This is really for you, Topo. After all, you haven't been . . . very happy with us. I think you know it yourself; this is the best thing for you."

The bewilderment on Topo's face deepened to a scowl and froze there.

"No way, I ain't going back to Ryerson!"

"Sh, sh, laddie," the Englishman begged.

"No goddamn way!" Topo hissed into Carleton's eyes and one of his thick fists pounded sharply against hte wall.

"This is just the thing I'm on about," Carleton cried. "No one can talk to you lad, there's no give and take. You can't get a handle on things and simply *talk*."

With a sudden kick, Topo sent a chair flying across the study and it clattered into a lamp. The room was too small, Carleton thought with a tremor, much too small!

Topo's eyes were flaming. "You promised me another chance; you promised!"

"I'd say you'd had your share of chances, Topo."

"You don't know anything that goes on around here,"

Topo spat. "You're walkin' around with your finger up your nose and you don't know anything!"

"That's enough!" Carleton cut him off. "You're still under my roof and you'll keep a civil tongue in your head while you are. Oh, I tried with you, lad . . ."

"Bull." Topo looked away in disgust. "You didn't try anything. You're no better than the rest of 'em, even though you think you are. You don't know what you're doing and we're the ones who gotta pay for it."

Carleton inhaled quickly, stung. Topo not only knew how to hurt, he knew *where*. Carleton wanted to fling something back, say something sharp and painful, but the words whirled out of his grasp. He was aware that sweat beaded on his upper lip and his eyes were blinking with it.

"You're leaving tomorrow." The Englishman struggled to keep both his voice and his legs steady. "Don't make me arrange an escort in blue."

Numbly, Topo left the study and slumped against the passage wall, aching. His eyes hurt and he closed them, his hair clinging damply to his forehead.

Even when it looked like it was getting better, Topo thought, even when it was getting to where maybe you could stand it, it got worse.

12

_____

"No way," Goat was saying gravely, "he won't live. He'll get shot and die because he's not a regular."

"Just watch," Marl said, hiking himself up on his elbows. "I think I've seen this one before."

Marl would always remember that the rec room smelled of soy sauce that night. Vilda had made her own Chinese food recipe: chicken strips, vegetables, and water chestnuts laced with soy sauce and strewn over rice. Even now, just after nine, the salty smell still hung in the hot air.

And it was hot. Marl kept wiping the dampness from his upper lip; Goat's white T-shirt was ringed with sweat. The most popular detective show of the season was on T.V. but Topo and Brucie were the only other boys who could stand the heat of the rec room. Everyone else was out on the porch or somewhere else cooler.

"Well, he could get wounded," Goat said doubtfully, "but he'll never walk again or anything. They'll go see him up in the hospital and meet up with his sister, or the guy who owns the nightclub."

Blam, blam! the television roared. Goat bounced cheerfully in his chair.

"See! I said he'd get shot."

"No, no, it's only his leg," Marl argued. "It's not serious. Look, he's still limping."

"Oh, pipe down," Topo grumbled. "Can't you guys ever shut up?"

Goat stiffened silently in his chair but Marl was feeling brave. Somehow, he wasn't afraid of Topo anymore—and he was still angry with him.

"What's wrong with you?" he asked, swinging around to glare at Topo. "You're always complaining about something, nothing's ever okay. You know, you should see a shrink. You really got problems."

It was the wrong thing to say to the wrong person. From under a lock of hair, Topo's eyes ignited.

"You miserable twerp," he started, pulling himself upright, "you goddamn . . ."

"Leave him alone." Goat didn't move; his eyes never left the screen.

"Oh, that's right, big man, you come and save your little boyfriend here."

Goat finally turned around. "What the? . . ."

"Problems?" Topo's eyes were burning into Marl. "You're the one who's got problems. You're screwed up so bad Jenner had to get somebody to baby-sit you."

"Shut up, Topo," Goat warned him, but the day's rage surged to the surface and the hefty boy was suddenly on his feet.

"Yeah, I heard him, I heard Jenner ask your hero here to look after you." Topo's voice raised an octave, crudely imitating Carleton's accent. "Be a good laddie and watch over little Marl for me, be his 'mate,' like."

"Shut up!" Goat lunged at Topo, shoving his shoulder hard. Topo staggered but quickly whirled back to face Goat.

"Can't take it, jerkface? Can't listen to the truth? You've been kissing Jenner's ass since you got here, and everybody's sick of it. Oh, they had you pegged at Ryerson, you got what you deserved. Now you think you're somebody again 'cause you got a little boyfriend to look after..."

With a strangled cry, Goat threw himself at Topo. They toppled to the rug, struggling while Brucie watched in horrified silence. Marl fled.

He flew past Carleton who was relaxing on the porch.

The Englishman jumped up and cried, "Wait!" but Marl was already into the night, quickly swallowed by the vast, dark prairie.

Oh, God. Marl was running, his arms swinging, his heart thudding. Oh, God! was all his mind could scream. He stumbled over the gnarled earth and fell, biting his lip painfully. He choked in some air and was up again, scrambling blindly.

When he couldn't run anymore, he loped. When he couldn't lope, he walked, holding his side. He wanted to throw up.

Baby-sitter! He should have known it was something like that. That's the way things always went for him. But he'd been so sure it was real! The day they'd worked on the bus, and last night, the report. Marl shivered, thinking of himself trying to read back what he'd written. Goat had listened so silently and every now and then he'd said, "Yeah, good," or "You got it." But maybe he'd been laughing inside!

A band tightened around Marl's throat and he glared at the stars over the horizon. He hated them, all of them! Trying to make you think this farm was okay when it was just as bad as everywhere else. It stunk, all of it.

"Never," he muttered; he'd never be taken in again. Nobody would ever get the chance! Marl's hands clenched into fists as he tramped determinedly over the stubble. This was the last time he would ever run away. This time, they wouldn't catch him.

The car lights lit up the highway like streamers. Marl stood on the edge of the field, just before the ditch, watching the cars, feeling the fury as they sped past. He knew what he'd do. He'd start walking towards town and if someone picked him up, he'd say he lived there, that he'd missed his ride back. Cecile had always told him that hitchhiking was dangerous, but so what! She didn't care. If she did, she would have taken him to live with her. But she didn't care and Marl didn't care. His life was one big, screwed-up mess and if some kind of crazy person picked him up, so what! If he made it to town, he'd run and keep on running.

The ache in his throat was so bad he had to blink before he swallowed. It wouldn't matter to anyone if he was gone. Not to Cecile or Jenner. Not to Goat.

Marl faced the direction of the farm. As if in a dream, he saw the distant glow of the yard lights.

"Don't think it bothers me." He flung the words at the night. "I don't care. I never did! I'm just gonna leave and you can all go to hell! I'm just gonna . . ."

Marl crumpled to the dry earth and began to sob.

"Vilda-a-a!"

She came, hair flying, hips bouncing, her eyes searching wildly for fire. There was no fire but she might have wished there was. Oh, how she hated scenes like this!

"Help me get them apart," Carleton cried, but Vilda had just taken a timid hold of Topo's shoulders when the boy gave Goat a fierce shove and they all went staggering backwards.

Carleton grasped Goat's wiry arms and Vilda held Topo's shoulders while the two boys swore violently at each other.

"Enough!" Carleton was shaking with rage. "Have done, already!"

Vilda glanced across at Goat's gray-blue eyes and shivered. She'd never seen such a cold blaze.

"What in God's name is going around here?" the Englishman demanded. "Every time I turn my back this house becomes a back alley brawl!"

Faces appeared at the rec room door, staring in curiously. Someone giggled. Carleton glared at Topo.

"But I can't say I'm surprised," he said grimly. "Lad, lad, this is just the kind of stunt that's sending you back to Ryerson."

The room became suddenly quiet.

"What?" Vilda asked softly, her fingers still clenching Topo's broad shoulders.

The Englishman nodded. "Aye, that's right, dear. He's leaving us tomorrow. I'm an understanding fellow but we can't have this sort of thing, day after day. After the way he attacked you, unprovoked, well, I couldn't take any chances."

Hearing this, Topo tore out of Vilda's grasp and threw himself on the couch, staring at the wall. Carleton's words settled on Vilda like sand.

"Dear Lord," she whispered. This wasn't supposed to happen! Topo, well, he wasn't as bad as all that. He was kinder, gentler than people knew, Vilda thought. And no one ever stood up for him.

"And you, Goat . . ." the Englishman was saying.

"Carl!" Vilda cut him off. The word seemed too loud and the heat rushed to Vilda's face. But it didn't matter, she had to tell him!

"He . . . it's not what you think. I'm trying to say . . ." Vilda stopped suddenly and looked around the room. "You all get along," she ordered. "We're havin' a private word here. All of you, go on!"

The boys had had more run-ins with Vilda than they'd ever had with Carleton. She was a tough lady and they knew it. Brucie scampered out of his chair and Topo followed with a backward glance. The others disappeared soundlessly, Goat moving with desperate speed.

Carleton folded his arms, trying to look in charge. "Now, what . . ."

"You sit," Vilda said briskly, "and you listen." A little miffed, Carleton sat.

"I think I've had a hand in what's troubling that poor boy," Vilda started. "At the canyon, I said some things that weren't real nice. If he's been acting up, I think it's 'cause his feelings are hurt."

"We've had problems for some time," Carleton began but Vilda shook her head with authority.

"I been a parent, I *know*," she said. "Besides, we had a talk, him and I. He's sorry for the way he's been."

101

"He has a strange way of showing it," Carleton said irritably.

"Well, nobody's perfect," Vilda said, "and boys are proud creatures. You mark my words; he'll come around."

She was a woman of strength and it was working for her now. Her composure rattled Carleton.

"But I've already made the arrangements. He's going! And besides," the Englishman defended himself, "there's too much here for one man. I can't . . . do the best job, with so many."

"So get help," Vilda said. Carleton looked at her as if she'd sworn at him.

"Help?"

"Yes, help," she said evenly. "Get one of them other social workers to live here. We've got enough space. Maybe you could get that nice Cecile lady, if she'd come."

"But, but . . ." Carleton sputtered.

"Remember those nice constables from town? They said they wanted to do something. Well, let 'em. Maybe they'd take the boys on field trips and the like."

"But I couldn't ask now!" Carleton pleaded and the cook looked at him with cold eyes.

"Hmph!" she sniffed. "Boys ain't the only ones who got pride. Well, you do what you like. Lord, I never went to school for this social working but I know selfish when I see it."

The word stunned Carleton like a stone.

"Selfish!" He pulled himself up as straight as a broom handle. "Why, I've devoted my life to children, spent years helping girls and lads like these. How could you say such a thing?"

"I don't know nothing about before," Vilda said, wiping her hands on her rumpled dress. "All I know about is now. Maybe they got another word for it, but what I'm seein' here I call selfish pride."

And she left then, her shoulders back and her dark hair fluttering. When she was out of sight she leaned against a wall and gasped.

What's come over you, old girl? she asked herself. She was trembling and as she laid her hand against her chest, she caught herself smiling just a bit. Maybe you couldn't fix the old wrongs, she thought, but you could do something about the ones you saw around you now.

Goat was flying. Each wiry leg reached out, straining, pulling him farther into the night. His lungs hurt, his calves ached, and each breath tore into his throat like sandpaper. He was a white stain on a black field.

This isn't like me, he thought. The panic, the cold fear, the fight with Topo. He felt as though he were watching someone else from a distance doing these weird things. It had come to him little by little over the past few weeks and now suddenly, here he was, running crazy over the fields. It wasn't like him at all! But he didn't stop.

When he heard Goat coming, Marl stood and wiped his eyes on his arms. He watched the white splash for some time: Goat's ragged breaths had disrupted the night like a dying train. The boy was ten meters away when he doubled forward, his hands on his bony knees, winded. Marl's own hands curled into defiant fists at his sides.

"What do you want?" he asked suspiciously.

Goat, still gasping, shook his head without looking up and spit.

"That's real sick, you know," Marl said, his lip curling in disgust.

Two more breaths and Goat raised his head, squinting. The moon was almost full and Marl noticed that the blond boy, the fields, and everything else were glossed with a silver sheen. It was ghostly, unreal, and it made him bold.

"What do you want?" he challenged again.

Goat was again walking towards him, swaying a little.

"Where you going?" he asked.

Marl's small, neat hands clenched tighter. "None of your business."

But Goat knew; he'd known as soon as Marl left the

farm. The boy had a history of running away when things went wrong. And parts of Marl, Goat realized, were so much like himself.

"Don't do it, kid," Goat said quietly, evenly. "You're just messing up your own life, real bad . . ."

"Screw you."

Goat's head jerked up, as if he'd bitten his tongue.

"Jenner tell you to say that too?" Marl's eyes glittered angrily. "Did he send you out here to bring me back, like some kinda watchdog? Well, you just go look after somebody else, big man, and score your points. But for Christ's sake, leave me alone. I'm sick of your good deeds."

The hard lines on Goat's face became even harder. "Now look . . ." he started and Marl turned away. "You listen to me!" Goat was seething. "Yeah, Topo got it right. Jenner asked me to watch your ass so you didn't get your teeth kicked in. And I was gonna tell him no, 'cause you know what? I don't need that shit. Everybody should just take care of themselves."

Marl's shoulders were very still.

"But then, I thought, what the hell, I'll give him a chance and I thought that maybe you weren't a bad kid. So I never wound up telling Jenner no. But I never told him yes!"

Marl made a half turn and looked at Goat sideways. The other boy took a deep breath and his voice softened.

"I never meant for this to happen. I never meant . . . for you to get hurt."

Marl's voice was cold. "What the hell do *you* know about hurt?"

Goat's arms twitched and his tight jaw set. Angrily he reached for the bottom of his T-shirt, then stopped. He glared at Marl for just a moment, then pulled it over his head with a quick tug. He felt the first rush of air against his skin and shivered in the hot night, gritting his teeth.

Marl stared. Goat was so painfully pale and gaunt that Marl felt a stab in his stomach. It took a while before he finally saw the scars.

They ran long and white on Goat's torso. Some criss-crossed like hideous train tracks and some were short and twisting, like gouges. Others were small and round, only the size of a fingernail. Eight years had not softened the grisly scene and nothing could have prepared Marl for it. He caught his breath.

Goat was standing, staring over Marl's head at the quiet prairie night sky. He could feel Marl's horror and he fought back the urge to tremble.

"Wanna see my back?" he asked softly.

"No," Marl whispered. "No."

Gratefully, Goat unclenched his shirt and pulled it on again. He'd never done that before, never shown himself willingly to anyone. He never wanted to again.

"Did . . . did you do that yourself?" Marl asked.

"Christ, no!"

His disgust hurt. Marl looked sharply away but the words slid out bitterly.

"Some people do," he said. There was a small pause; Goat's fingers curled into his palms.

"You?" Goat asked carefully.

Marl shrugged. He wasn't going to tell right now. He'd told enough about himself. It was Goat's turn.

"Is that what Topo meant about Ryerson?" It was a question, but it sounded like a dare.

Goat bit the inside of his lip. "No, I got those before. This," he pointed to the long scar on the side of his face, "I got at Ryerson. And this," he pulled back the neck of his shirt. "And this."

"How?" Marl pushed. Goat shrugged and sighed.

"Oh, you know. Fighting and stuff." His voice lowered. "I guess I really was playing big man or something. After a while, some guys sorta got me back. In the showers, by the gym. After that, they put me in closed custody. I guess they thought I was really crazy."

Marl shut his eyes but it was too late. He'd been to Ryerson. He could see the showers Goat was talking about. He knew how easy it would be to corner someone there, and how hard the tile floors were. The whole night seemed raw with pain.

Everybody, Marl thought, everybody's got scars. They were what happened to you on the road from there to here. Some scars you could see and some you couldn't. That was the only difference.

Marl opened his eyes cautiously. They stung and watered. He remembered Topo and the empty, empty bag.

"I gotta go," he sniffed.

"Why?"

Marl shrugged but it looked like a tremor. "I can't go back, not now. Everybody knows. . . what happened. They're all laughing at me."

"Come on, nobody knows," Goat said, scuffing impatiently at the dirt. "And even if they did, they wouldn't care. It doesn't matter."

Marl felt a jab of anger in his side. "Well, *I* know," he said sharply, "and it matters to me."

He leapt down into the ditch that ran alongside the highway and then bounded up onto the asphalt. The moon was bright but the road felt dangerous, as if he could feel the rumble of distant cars. Far away there was a light and Marl was just about to wonder what it was when he heard the soft swish, swish of the grass.

"Okay," Goat muttered, "all right, you go. You go and screw up your life and have a good time at it."

He was leaving! Marl realized with a pang. Goat was really going. He wasn't going to ask Marl to stay, not even one more time!

Numbly, Marl listened to the determined crushing of crabgrass. It was getting softer as Goat moved farther and farther away. Then, Marl heard something else.

"You know, I really thought you were okay!" The voice was faded over the prairie. "I really thought you were my friend!"

Marl searched the night, his eyes catching the stark white T-shirt and the glint of Goat's blond hair.

"But I was wrong," the voice continued, wavering. "You

don't care. What I did for you, I never did for nobody! Now you can't even go back and look Jenner in the eye. You're a coward, coward! Yeah, you run and you keep running. Nobody's going to miss you, not ever!"

He spun around angrily and continued walking away, his hands shoved into his pockets, his shoulders hunched.

Marl whirled back to the highway and the light on his face caught him like a blow. It had come up suddenly, a single deadly beam that froze him with fear. The terrible dream was coming true! His stomach lurched, the ground had the sickly sway of a train running too fast. The light zoomed closer and closer but Marl couldn't stop it. He was helpless! A horn was blasting but he couldn't move. It was the horrible end he had always expected!

"Goat!" Marl screamed. "For God's sake, Goat!"

The scream broke the spell. Marl dived from the highway, rolling into the ditch, and the 1971 Pontiac Fury with the burned-out headlight sped past, whipping the tall grass.

"Damn deer," the driver grumbled. "Coulda wrecked my front end."

Marl's strength came rushing back. He leapt out of the ditch and sprinted after the thin figure on the prairie.

"Goat!" Marl cried again and the white T-shirt slowed, but didn't stop. Something wet in his eyes was blinding Marl but he kept scrambling, feeling stronger with every step. When at last he caught up with the other boy, Marl was choking and sputtering but he felt he was finally safe. He was off the road and he was safe.

"Christ," Goat muttered, "what were you trying to do? Get yourself killed?"

"I . . . I . . ." Marl gasped, but Goat stopped him with a shrug. He couldn't look at Marl because he was embarrassed by the feeling in him. It was so big that he was silent for a few minutes as they trudged across the grass.

"Thanks," was all that Goat said when he could talk, but it was enough. Friends always know what you really mean.

13

At the first jangle of the telephone, Cecile was awake and frightened. She knew instinctively that it was too early for good news: Good news could always wait until a decent hour and it was only just after 7 A.M. now. In one panicky lunge she dived and caught the villain on its second ring.

"What?" she demanded breathlessly into the receiver.

The caller on the other end was taken aback. He'd forgotten that some people spent their nights sleeping, not pacing.

"Cecile, dear," Carleton said at last, "glad I caught you before you left. What time does your plane leave, by the way?"

"What?" she asked again, irritated by his good mood and his small talk.

"Oh, ahem," the Englishman coughed nervously, and he knew there could be no stalling, not now.

"Cecile, I need . . . I mean, I have an idea," he began. As he talked, Cecile sat up, listening and staring as if she could see him through the wire.

"This is so sudden," she said, the blankets clutched up to her chest.

"Well, I wanted to catch you before your holidays, in case you needed time to think. I understand this would mean a career change for you. And really, it's different work than . . . what you're used to."

Excitement fluttered like a tiny moth in Cecile's chest, but she tried to stay calm and behave like the cool professional she was supposed to be. It would be a different life with Carleton and the boys on the Jenner farm. She'd be stranded out in the Badlands with a bunch who could be wild sometimes. But oh, to be with Marl and watch him grow!

Her stomach suddenly plummeted. She was doing it again, wasn't she? She was being possessive about Marl. If it was affecting her so much now, what would happen if she was living in the same house with him? How could she possibly remain fair?

Cecile sighed.

"I find your offer very interesting, Carl, but I'm not sure I'm your best choice."

"What do you mean?" the Englishman asked, his voice hushed with concern.

"To be perfectly honest, I'm not completely impartial sometimes . . . and that could be a problem."

"Marl?" Carleton asked.

"Yes, Marl."

Now it was Carleton's turn to sigh. "The world asks a lot of us, doesn't it, Cecile? We're supposed to genuinely care about these children, but not love any of them. Or dislike any of them. We're not supposed to be human."

Listening, Cecile found herself nodding, her eyes filling with sudden, surprised tears.

"As you may have guessed this . . . possessiveness is a problem for me, too," Carleton admitted, his voice just above a whisper. "We all want to be completely fair all the time but . . ." He trailed off and there was a pause. "Well, you could watch me and I could watch you," Carleton said.

Cecile swallowed the knot in her throat. He was offering to help her if she would help him. She was touched and grateful.

"I'd love to give it a try," Cecile said. "Just give me these two weeks of holidays as a breather, time to prepare myself. I'll start making arrangements as soon as I get back."

"Good show!" Carleton said heartily. "And thank you. I'm really looking forward to working with you."

"Thank you," Cecile replied gently, calm now that she had made her decision.

The thing was in motion! Carleton marveled as he hung up the phone. He hadn't thought he could do it, but here it was, begun. There was only one dark spot on this bright new horizon and it came in the shape of a lumbering, brooding boy.

The plans are already made, Carleton said to himself. There's no backing out now. Yet he felt a sharp twinge between his shoulder blades as he stood up.

On a real farm, the boys would have been up long before breakfast. But here there were no animals to feed and eight o'clock was early enough. Too early, some thought. Carleton bounded from door to door, clapping each with the flat of his hand.

"Rise and shine, lads!" he sang briskly. "Uppity up! It's a fine day."

In one of the rooms, Rayo moaned.

"God, he's so weird," another voice grumbled and the figures began to shift and stir sleepily. Marl was awake, wide awake, but he lay quietly even as the room was coming to life.

It was the feeling of safety and stillness that amazed him. The whole world seemed bolted down at last. His back welcomed the steady bed the way your feet welcome the ground after a long, dizzy roller coaster ride. What a feeling it was, to have his own bed, his own pillows! And downstairs, someone was making breakfast, *his* breakfast, and he would sit at his own spot at the table, two chairs over from Goat. It had been a long, dangerous road, Marl thought, but now that he was here, it was okay. This place, this farm with its people, was his place.

A hand shook his shoulder.

"Come on," Brucie said gravely, "or you won't get any."

When he was gone, Marl threw back the covers and jumped up into the day, the hopeful sun as warm as love on his naked back.

"He's going, you know," Goat said casually.

"Who?" Marl asked. It was after breakfast and the two boys were alone in the kitchen on clean up duty. Goat was up to his elbows in suds and Marl was stacking dirty plates, a dish towel slung over his arm.

"Topo," Goat said, swishing water around a mixing bowl, "back to Ryerson. Jenner said so last night."

Topo, back to Ryerson. Marl repeated the words in his head. He expected to feel a gush of relief but it didn't come. Last night he'd hated Topo, hated his guts! But today was a whole world away from last night. Marl felt a twinge between his shoulder blades.

"Ryerson stinks," he said.

"I know," Goat sighed. "I been there, remember?"

Marl leaned against the counter. "Nobody deserves Ryerson. Not even Topo."

Goat looked at him with strange, surprised eyes, as if Marl was crazy. "What?" he said, his eyebrows furrowing.

A week ago, Marl would have backed down. But today he was strong. In the light of the morning kitchen he was feeling safe and normal and strong. "We gotta do something," he said.

Goat snorted and reached for the gray broiler pan. "Not me; it's none of my business," he said beginning to scrub. "Let him go."

"Christ!" Marl's dishes banged as he dumped them on the counter. "What's the matter with you? Don't you care about anybody except yourself?"

Goat straightened, stung.

"Grow up," Marl threw the words out. "You know what that place is like. It's no big deal to see if we can do something. God, we live here," he motioned to include to the whole farm, "but we're not completely out of it. We're not retarded or anything."

In a way, Marl couldn't believe the sound of the words in his ears. Was he actually saying these things? He must have been: Goat was staring at him in surprised awe. Then Goat looked away, a pink heat rising to his face. He attacked the silverware as if it were an enemy, making it clatter as he dropped it into the tray to drain.

"Okay, so what's your great idea?" he muttered.

Marl ran his hand through his thick, dark hair. "I don't know. Let's go talk to Jenner or something. Maybe he doesn't know what it's like there. Maybe he'll change his mind."

They worked quietly for a moment until Goat looked up, a shy smile curling his lips.

"You better be careful," he teased, "or you'll wind up a social worker or something."

Marl dunked his hand in the sink and a stream of suds caught Goat across the neck.

They found Carleton Jenner in the study. For Carleton, it was a bad time: He and Vilda were just discussing what could possibly be done about Topo and the cook had the Englishman cornered.

"Yes?" Carleton said irritably. "What is it, Marl?"

The boy stepped forward although Goat hung back, just inside the door. Marl was embarrassed to find everyone staring at him and his face flushed with heat. But he pushed on.

"Mr. Jenner? I hear you got Topo going back to Ryerson," Marl said.

"Yes, that's right."

"I . . . I don't think you want to do that," the boy said. Carleton threw up his hands.

"Good grief! Why does everyone want to run this farm all of a sudden?" he exclaimed, but Vilda cut him off.

"There! That's just what I been sayin'," Vilda pointed

at Marl. "I'm not the only one who thinks that way. You go on, Marl, you tell 'em why."

Marl glaced back at Goat, whose mouth was clamped shut. The boy with the almond eyes swallowed.

"It's not a good place for a kid to grow up in," he said quietly. "You can get kinda lost. Even if you want things to work out, you can get off the right track, you know?"

Vilda's hands were on her hips, triumphant. "I been sayin' the same thing, right here in this room. You listen to that boy, Carl!"

"Oh, bloody hell," the Englishman muttered. "The arrangements are already made. What can I do now?"

Vilda had thought about that. "You get Topo to call that director *himself*," she said. "He'll tell her why he deserves to stay himself, and we'll see what she says to that."

"You think it might work?" Carleton asked, chewing on the end of a pen.

"Yeah," there was a creak in his voice and Goat coughed. "Yeah. I know the director pretty good. She might go for it."

Carleton sighed and pointed the end of his pen at Marl.

"All right, lads, on your insistence we'll give it a go. But . . ." he shook the pen for emphasis, "if he stays and doesn't honestly *try*, I won't be this generous again."

Leaning against a filing cabinet, Vilda smiled.

When Marl and Goat had left the study, they walked quietly down the hallway. Just before they reached the kitchen, Goat stopped. He was looking at Marl, biting his lip and wondering. Marl felt the question.

"What?" he said.

Goat paused. "Why'd you do it?"

"Do what?"

Goat jerked his head towards the study. "That. For Topo."

"I don't know," Marl shrugged. He stuck his hands in his pockets and kept walking through the kitchen towards the door. Goat leapt to catch up.

113

"No, really. Why?" he said again, stopping Marl with a hand on his shoulder, just in front of the screen.

Marl took a deep breath.

"I . . . I been there, I guess," Marl said, looking out. "On that road. Sometimes you need a little push, to get off."

Goat looked at him for a moment, his rainy-sea eyes open and clear. Then the scar disappeared in a crease.

"Right, social worker, and here's one for you!" He lunged and a friendly shoulder check sent Marl sprawling through the screen door, laughing onto the prairie.